F IS FOR FETISH

Also by Alison Tyler

———

Best Bondage Erotica

Best Bondage Erotica 2

Exposed

The Happy Birthday Book of Erotica

Heat Wave: Sizzling Sex Stories

Luscious: Stories of Anal Eroticism

The Merry XXXmas Book of Erotica

Red Hot Erotica

Slave to Love

Three-Way

Caught Looking (with Rachel Kramer Bussel)

A Is for Amour

B Is for Bondage

C Is for Coeds

D Is for Dress-Up

E Is for Exotic

G Is for Games

H Is for Hardcore

F IS FOR FETISH

EROTIC STORIES
EDITED BY ALISON TYLER

CLEIS
PRESS

Published in the United States by Cleis Press Inc.,
P.O. Box 14697, San Francisco, California 94114.

Printed in the United States.
Cover design: Scott Idleman
Text design: Karen Quigg
Cleis Press logo art: Juana Alicia
First Edition.
10 9 8 7 6 5 4 3 2 1

ACKNOWLEDGMENTS

Ferocious fondness to my fierce friends:

Adam Nevill

Felice Newman

Frédérique Delacoste

Diane Levinson

Violet Blue

the Lust Bites Ladies

and SAM, always.

Nothing risqué, nothing gained.

—ALEXANDER WOOLLCOTT

contents

INTRODUCTION:
FEEL FREE...

EEL FREE TO IMAGINE ME FULLY FLUSHED HERE…because reading the stories for *F Is for Fetish* turned me pink cheeked from start to finish. I should have known, I suppose, that *this* would be the theme that would generate the most widespread response, from writers obsessed by everything from fingers to toes and fishnets to dildos.

What do *I* know about fetishes?

Plenty. I have been a fan of leather since my freshman year at college. My friend Alana sat in front of me in History and she'd saved up all of her summer job money to buy a leather jacket with a fur collar. (Yeah, she was one of those wise-beyond-her-years types.) She wore the jacket all fall and winter, and she accentuated the natural scent of the leather with Obsession perfume. I sat behind her and missed every lecture, stroking the skin of her jacket and drinking in her scent. Her scent mixed with the smell of the hide.

But maybe my fetish began before that, on a trip to Manhattan just before college, when my parents' friend Simone took me to a show her friends were in. Four of us shared the back of a cab, and three were in leather pants: Simone, her friend Michael, his lover David. I was surrounded by the butter-soft material, surrounded by that most sensual aroma ever.

I've never gotten over the way I feel when wearing leather, when touched with leather gloves, when zipped up tight in an ankle-length leather jacket. And that sensation is akin to the way I felt when reading these stories. The very heady scent of sex flooded over me as I turned the pages dedicated to fingers (Shanna Germain) and toes (Stan Kent), boots (Kristina Lloyd) and bad girls (Barbara Pizio). I reveled in fetishes I adore—bondage, voyeurism, spanking—and learned about some brand-new ones. And as I read the words, each fetish came alive to me, swept over me, left me breathless and blushing.

So as I said, feel free...feel free to imagine me flushed. And feel free to turn crimson-cheeked yourself as you dive into the frisky fetishes described in these fourteen flirty fables.

XXX,
Alison Tyler

SHANNA GERMAIN

KNUCKLING UNDER

FINGERS. They do me in every time. Not eyes or a smile, not shoulders or calves, but fingers. I could be such a good girl, could keep my libido where it belongs, if it weren't for those fingers, promising to work their magic.

That time, it was my bike mechanic's fingers that I was lusting for. His fingers were muscular somehow. Each one was squared off at the tip, with a big, flat nail. Bits of bicycle grease filled the whorls of his knuckles and lined the edges of his fingernails.

The rest of him wasn't bad either, like those chocolate eyes that I noticed right off. And then that just-long-enough curly dark hair. He had the body of a cyclist, lean and muscular in his jeans and blue T-shirt.

But there are lots of men who look like that. I'd resisted them. I thought I could resist him. He could have been just a pleasant daydream as I stood in line, my bike leaning on my hip, waiting for the woman in front of me to finish. He didn't raise his eyes much, and it gave me a chance to watch him, to imagine what it would be like to seduce him, take him home. Just a dream, a way to pass the time.

I'd gotten pretty far in my daydream—to the point where he had hiked up my short work skirt and was running one finger up the inside of my thigh—by the time it was my turn. I stepped up to the counter with my bike in tow.

Nice smile, but shy. He didn't say anything, which he could only pull off because he was so adorable. He didn't even really take his eyes off my bike. You could tell he was more comfortable with bikes than people. But at least he didn't notice that I was wheeling my bike in while dressed in heels and my office ensemble, while all the others were sporting their padded bike shorts and SuperFabric shirts. I'd had a hell of a time getting it out of the car, trying not to ruin my panty hose since I had to go back to work.

"I have a flat," I said.

I was kind of embarrassed to admit that I'd brought my bike to the shop for a flat tire, but the truth is I'm not a bike geek. I like to ride, but I don't really understand how bikes work. I can't change my own tire. I'd been telling myself that I was going to take a class and learn the basics. He'd just shot my incentive all to hell.

He motioned toward one of the rails behind the counter. "Why don't you bring it around back?" he said.

I wheeled my bike around the edge of the counter. He took it from me and put it up on the rails. And that's when I saw his fingers, really saw them, for the first time. All that grease. A certain strength in the knuckles that comes from working with your hands. But his skin wasn't cut or chapped, and the grease was new. Like he went home every night and washed every bit of work from his hands, took care of them. It was that combination that got me. My light crush turned into a full-out throb that beat steady inside my underwear.

He caressed the curves of my bike with the pads of his fingers. My skin ached with longing. For once, I was jealous of my bike—I wanted those fingers on me, not on her.

"Nice bike," he said.

She *was* a nice bike. Specialized, all white, unisex frame. A gift from my husband, who'd named her The White Goose. He called me *Saraswathi*, after the Hindu goddess of wisdom who rides a white goose, so it seemed appropriate. Only *Saraswathi* is supposed to represent purity itself. And here I was, doing—or dreaming of doing—just the opposite.

He ran those perfect fingers along the bike's curves and let them linger in her hidden spots. He pressed his fingers in the gear spots where she always wanted more oil, tucked them into the corner of the stem that always collected dirt. I'd always wanted a man like that, who could discover my hidden places and know intuitively how I wanted, needed, to be touched. Not sex, but something else. Discovery maybe. Or the feeling that someone knows you better than you do yourself.

Watching his fingers made me dizzy. The smooth sound of his skin sliding over her frame, the way he tucked his fingertips beneath the lip of the seat—it was too much. Then he moved down to the flat tire. While he spun the wheel with one hand, he kept two fingers pressed to the side of the wheel. The sound was a steady slide, like someone pulling a skirt up over stockinged thighs.

"Aha," he said. "Here's your problem."

When he found the blowout spot, he dug in, pulling the cut bit of tire open. I wanted his fingers on me like that, sliding across me, opening me up.

"Looks like you hit a nice chunk of glass," he said. He held out a triangle-shaped piece of green glass as though he were offering it to me. Its sharp edges made his fingers look dangerous. "The tire should be okay, but you'll need a new tube."

He dropped the glass on the counter and picked up a long black tool. The way his fingers molded around the handle made the tool an extension of his hand. I wondered if you could learn a body like that, as though it was part of you. Every movement, every touch, more instinct than thought. He brought the tool toward my tire, and then seemed to realize I was still standing there, watching.

"It'll only take me a couple of minutes. You can wait if you want to."

I said something witty like, "Could you tell me where the restroom is?" and then backed away, trying to pretend I wasn't still looking at his fingers.

In the employee restroom, I talked to the mirror. "You will not do this," I told my reflection. My reflection listened and nodded. Always the good girl. But my reflection's eyes were alive, shining in a way that she couldn't hide. And that corner of her lip tilted up. I knew that neither of us was listening to my little speech.

I kept going anyway. I listed all the ways my husband was a good man: sexy, kind, willing to put up with all of my shit. I didn't let myself think about his hands. He had long, thin fingers. Soft as kid gloves. When he touched me, it was with long, soft strokes, like I was made of marzipan. Even when he put his fingers inside me, it was never more than two, never enough to stretch my body open. His fingers soothed, aroused. But never pressed, never opened me as far as I wanted him to. Never bruised.

I could resist this man. I would. And besides, he hadn't even noticed me. Didn't notice anything except my bike. Wasn't interested in me. At all.

It was this realization that allowed me to grasp the doorknob to let myself out of the restroom. If I couldn't resist of my own accord, I would let his lack of interest do it for me. I would take my bike and go back to work. And tonight I would ride, pressing myself hard against the seat, thinking of his fingers.

I opened the door and stepped out, and there he was. Leaning against the hall wall, looking down at his shoes. His hands were tucked in his apron pockets. Without his fingers, he was avoidable. That's what allowed me to smile. To say something sharp and witty like, "Oh, sorry, I didn't know you were waiting."

He took his hands from his apron pockets and used them to push back his dark curls. One snagged on the meat of his finger, refusing to let go. It gave me a glimpse of how it would be to look down and see his finger wrapping itself in my own dark curls.

I tried to swallow or look away, but my muscles refused to obey. Every part of my body wanted to lean toward him, magnetized. I had one hand still on the doorknob. I don't know where my other hand was.

He looked up at me for the first time, those big brown eyes deep pools in his face.

"It's your calves," he said.

My hand on the doorknob was doing a weird twisty thing that I couldn't seem to control. "I'm sorry?" I said.

His fingers drifted back to his hair, pulling at a curl.

"I have a girlfriend, so I tried not to look," he said. "Tried not to, but I couldn't help it…"

His voice trailed away and he bit his lower lip with his two top teeth, perfect squares against the pink flesh. When he looked back down, I realized he hadn't been looking at the floor or my bike all this time. He'd been looking at my legs.

I knew then that I wasn't the only one with a fetish, and that realization allowed me to feel strong. I lifted my head—I would slip by him, let him into the bathroom and let myself out the front door. I would pay whoever needed to be paid and I'd find another bike mechanic; a fat, ugly one with stubby little fingers.

As I moved, he put one finger out, like he was going to press an elevator button. I don't know if he meant to push the door open. Or maybe he meant to touch me on the shoulder. Either way, his finger ended up against my bottom lip. I tasted metal and grease and clean skin. I wanted to suck his finger into my mouth, to feel his calluses between my teeth. My tongue ran over the tip. The contrast between the smooth nail and the bits of rough skin at the edges took away the last of my resolve.

I sucked his finger into my mouth, held it there. He made a sound in the back of his throat, a low hum that made my belly contract. Keeping my lips tight around his finger, I led him backward into the restroom.

He let me lead him like that, and the door shut behind us, closing us into the small space. I let go of his finger, and he reached behind to lock the door. His hands moved quickly—fast and hard on my ass, on my thighs—and before I could even register it, he was lifting me up, setting me on the edge of the sink.

My skirt and his fingers made slippery sounds as he pushed the fabric up until my thighs were exposed. He put his hands between my legs, opened them until he could fit his body between.

I didn't know how to tell him what I wanted. It wasn't sex. It was those hands, those fingers.

Maybe he already knew. Maybe he'd realized my fetish when I'd sucked his finger into my mouth, because he put one hand up, smeared it roughly across my mouth like he was wiping away old lipstick. I caught one finger between my teeth on the way by, but he shook free, and closed his fingers around my chin. He tilted my head down, made me watch as he used his other hand to press into my thighs, to scratch at my panty hose until small runs appeared.

He let go of my chin, but I went on watching. His fingers made a small tear in the fabric, and then another, longer. Where he'd made the hole, his warm skin brushed mine. He burrowed his fingers beneath the fabric. I loved the way his hands looked, trapped under the see-through black, pressing hard into my skin.

His fingers grabbed the center of my thong and pushed it aside. And then his fingers wrapped themselves in my curls, twisting and tugging. The contrast of my dark hair with his skin made it hard to breathe. Without waiting, he put his fingers inside me. Hard. Just like I'd hoped. I couldn't tell how many—two at least, maybe three. I was already wet, but the feel of his calluses lightly scratching the inside of me made me wetter.

He thrust his fingers into me, using his whole body, shoving my hips back and forth across the porcelain. I wrapped my calves around his back, and he made that low hum again in the back of his throat.

I couldn't watch anymore. The feeling of it made me want to come, but watching his fingers fuck me was throwing me over the edge. I didn't want to come yet, so I closed my eyes and leaned back against the mirror. My reflection had turned her back on me, but I didn't care anymore. I just wanted him to keep touching me the way he was doing.

"Watch," he said, his voice low. It was a whisper, but it was also a command. I opened my eyes.

He took his fingers out of me and ran them, wet and glistening, down the inside of my thigh. Then he folded his hand, four fingers forming a point, and entered me once more. I watched as he pushed, slow but not gentle, inside me. He found my clit with his thumb, rubbed it hard enough to make me cry out, and then flicked at it with a fingernail. It was one second of pain and three of pleasure. And then it was all pleasure: watching his fingers move in and out of me, feeling the sharp edge of his thumb flicking in time to his strokes.

He reached back and wrapped his free hand around my calf muscle. His fingers dug in, and I tightened my legs around his back, made my calf muscles taut.

"Put your legs up," he said, ducking down a little, his fingers never stopping their steady movement. I put my legs over his shoulders. The lip of the sink dug into my back, but I could barely feel it. All my nerve endings were working overtime around his fingers. There wasn't room to feel anything else.

"Tighter," he said. I flexed my calves against his neck muscles. I wanted to reach down and touch him, to help him get off, but he seemed as focused on my calves as I was on his fingers, and I thought maybe he didn't want anything else.

He curled his fingers inside me—*come-hither*—once, twice against my G-spot, and I didn't think anymore. I just closed my eyes and focused on his touch. Thumb flicking my clit. Fingertips hitting that sponge spot that made my body feel all shivery.

My orgasm was as fast and hard as his fingers, rushing through me and then gone. He kept his fingers in, let me spasm around him until my body was still.

When he removed his fingers I felt empty, split open. I took my legs off his shoulders, surprised at how heavy they felt, how tired I was. The whole room smelled like grease and salt. I realized he was still dressed, that I'd hardly touched him. That he hadn't come.

I reached for his zipper, but he stopped my hands. His fingers were still wet from me.

"It's okay," he said. He put one finger on my ripped panty hose and ran it down to my calf. It left a glistening trail on the black. "I got just what I wanted. Plus, I have to go back and finish your bike."

I'd forgotten about the bike. Actually, for three or five or ten minutes, I'd forgotten about everything. Now, watching him reach for a paper towel to dry his fingers, it all came back. My promise to be a good girl. To keep my libido in check. To be true to my husband.

But you can't help what you love. Or what you lust after. And those fingers; those strong, sexy fingers; they get me every time.

NIKKI MaGennis

HaIR TRIGGER

FRANKIE CAME OUT OF NOWHERE.

In the bar where they met for the first time, he beckoned Sal over to where he sat—a booth in the quiet section. He had a lavish smile, and blew smoke around them as he talked, so that the dark corner of the pub filled with a blue haze.

"You're beautiful, did you know that?"

Sal smiled, and sat down. She took a sip of her gin-and-soda, held the ice cube in her mouth until there was nothing left but a cold, sharp sliver.

"But I'd be more beautiful naked, right?"

"Perhaps. Actually, I was thinking I wanted to see you with your hair down."

Automatically, Sal's hand flew to her hair. That night she'd straightened it, rubbed wax into the tips, and swept it up into a chignon. A few loose strands swam around her face.

"Why don't you take it down, sugar?"

Sal crunched the ice sliver in her mouth. Locking her eyes on his, she reached up and pulled out the clip. Her hair tumbled loose, a long black curtain falling to the small of her back.

"Much better." He nodded. "Now, let's talk about the naked part."

He leaned forward, hands nearly touching Sal's on the tabletop.

When he reached out finally to touch her, to pull one lock of hair between his fingers, she knew what would happen next. Still, she loved the anticipation, how the atmosphere grew heavy and shimmered with wanting.

"What are you doing Friday night?" he asked.

On Friday Sal waited for him. Her door buzzer went off at precisely eight thirty, and she jumped like she'd had an electric shock. She forced herself not to run to answer it, tried to keep the shake out of her voice as she spoke.

"Hello?"

"Rapunzel, Rapunzel, let down your hair," he said.

Within an hour they were in bed.

It became their Friday game. As he asked, every week Sal wore her hair up, perfumed and shined with serum, artfully tangled. She dressed in elaborate outfits: stockings, basques, lace-trimmed slips. High heels and immaculate makeup, ribbons and hooks and small pearl buttons. Frankie liked her prepared like this, so carefully primped. Ready for him to unravel.

He'd arrive at eight thirty precisely. Never early, never late.

Sometimes Sal would suggest they go out for dinner, catch a movie, but Frankie brushed her ideas aside.

"Let's just stay in," he said. "I prefer you naked."

After a few weeks, she stopped suggesting they do anything else. After all, she was as hooked on their Friday night game as he was. She burned with the tension of waiting. Each time the week swung round to Friday, she felt the dark, strange magic of their ritual take hold. It was like a drumbeat that echoed faintly in the background all the time, even when she couldn't hear it, until the end of the week, when the rhythm would start to pound. By eight thirty, she was deafened by the noise.

She'd fixed her hair with pins, and a couple of black enamel combs. When he said the word she turned to the gilt-framed mirror over the table. She knew he liked to watch her, pins in her mouth, arms raised, undoing her hair so it fell around her shoulders. And she'd watch him in the mirror, his eyes following the long trail of her hair reaching halfway down her back. She shook it free. The smell of coconut filled the room.

Still standing in front of the mirror, she waited.

"Strip."

Her hands shook as she fumbled over her buttons and wriggled out of her clothes. She let them fall at her feet—kicked aside the puddles of cloth to stand naked before him. He didn't allow her to cover herself.

"Keep your hands at your sides."

She knew he liked the contrast—dark hair, pale skin. The parts of her that never saw daylight, they were the parts he liked the best.

That's where he'd linger, with his hands and his tongue and his teeth. He'd stroke her long neck and the delicate skin on the underside of her arm. The crease of her breasts. Her sex.

She shaved herself so smooth and hairless her pubis was as soft as soap to the touch. A small tuft covered her clit, just enough for him to tug at with his long piano-player's fingers. After a few days, she'd get a rash and the small hairs would grow back red and angry, but oh, God it was worth it for Friday nights. To see how his eyes would darken. To feel those soft lips press against her bare pussy.

When they fucked he held her down, slid into her like a knife, moved so slowly she felt herself falling into a deep and endless space. It was sex like the night sky, silent and expansive. And his skin—his honey-colored skin—was taut and perfect. He pressed himself against her and they were two leaves of damp paper, stuck fast together. Cleaving.

When it came, the orgasm broke them apart, a supernova rending the universe: white-hot; cold and dazzling. Sal spun out into the void, alone in her private blissworld. As though she ceased to exist for a few moments, she was elsewhere. Blank, yet ecstatic.

Afterward, they lay in a ruck of damp sheets with his hands tangled in her hair, his mouth against her ear whispering words she couldn't hear.

She should have picked up on the warnings, of course, but who can really tell danger from exhilaration? She had nightmares: grotesque animals spilling out of closets; electric cables wrapping round her ankles; phone calls with nobody on the other end of the line. She'd wake up gasping.

Two, three months passed. Without her noticing, the landscape of Sal's life changed. It was as though a curtain was pulled over her weekends. Fridays were inviolate, a sacred ritual. Her weekly dose of Frankie's adoration doled out in one sweet, concentrated night.

Afterward, when they slept, he'd wrap himself in her hair, as though they were bound together, as though they were weaving a subtle net around the hours of sleep. Sal felt him bury himself in the crook of her neck and wondered if he was as trapped as she was.

The rest of the week grew colorless compared to Fridays. Sal went out less, telling herself she needed rest to recover from the intensity of the weekend games. She wouldn't admit the real reason—she was waiting for his out-of-the-blue phone call. She should have known. He called on Thursdays, at seven sharp. Never early, never late. Week after week, his ritual never varied. Yet she waited, hovered, hoped.

The night she turned up at his flat unannounced, overnight bag trailing behind her like a cumbersome pet, she wore her sheerest black top, a tight pair of culottes, and silk underwear. She'd chosen the ferociously high heels, the ones that made her walk with tiny little steps, ass thrust out, hips swaying.

His eyes narrowed when he opened the door. It was a Wednesday. They weren't scheduled.

He was in a suit—shirt open at the neck, phone in his hand.

"What's wrong?" he asked, eyes flicking to the stairwell behind her.

"Nothing," she said, smiling. "Just wanted to see you."

Inside, her heart was shrinking and leaping at the same time. The smile was plastered to her face. She stood there holding the strap of her bag and felt like a door-to-door salesman, begging for a little time. Behind him, the light in his hall was yellow and warm, spilling out the door.

"Didn't you think of phoning?" he asked, holding the door half-open.

She shook her head, and then in a moment of inspiration, reached up to pull the clip out of her hair. She sighed, like she'd had a hard day. Shook her hair out.

"I've had a hard day," she said. "Gonna let me in?"

A split second too long passed. The smell of coconut hung in the air between them.

"Sure," he said, stepping back.

Frankie's flat was unknown territory. Her heels clattered on the polished floor as she followed him, padding barefoot in front of her. He showed her into the kitchen, poured a glass of tap water, and left her.

"I have to take a shower," he said.

Sal sat and stared at the pistachio green walls. She heard the lock on the bathroom door slide shut, and then the faint hiss of the shower. The kitchen was sparse. There was checkered linoleum on the floor and strip lighting overhead. A jar on the counter held whisks, cooking spoons and scissors. Pinned to the wall, an art calendar showed Venus coming out of the sea, her face sweet and perfect. Underneath dates were marks in different colored pen; red crosses and black crosses. Sal stared at his coded dates and shifted in her seat. The shoes were pinching her feet.

Hit by a flash of queasy inspiration, she slipped out of her high heels. In stockinged feet, she crept into the hall and checked the closed doors. Like a cat burglar, she considered her options, and finally pushed open the door at the end of the hall.

His bed was large, and sat in the middle of the room. The covers were messed up. She always thought of Frankie as obsessively neat, and the sight of his unmade bed gave her a pang of tender feelings, as though she'd caught a glimpse of some secret folded in among the creases of white linen.

Moving fast, she stripped off her top and culottes, and placed them in a pile on a chair. In her whore's underwear, she climbed into Frankie's bed, and lay on top of the rumpled covers. Her daring excited her, and she felt the welcome rush and tingle between her thighs as she grew wet.

Sal took a deep breath—and noticed a scent clinging to the sheets. A sweet, bitter and musky smell, something both familiar and strange. When she pulled back the covers, it rose up into her nostrils, and she breathed in the scent of another woman: her perfume, her sex. Curled across the pillow was a long, fine red hair. Sal picked it up and held it between her fingers, mesmerized.

Frankie opened the door, skin still damp from the shower, a towel wrapped loosely round his hips.

"Fuck," he said under his breath. "You're beautiful."

He walked to her, and pushed his fingers into her hair, pulled her to him to kiss her long and deep. Sal felt the wonderful softness of his lips, his warm, wet mouth, the heat of his skin.

She pulled away. Stood up.

"Lie down, Frankie," she said.

"You're giving orders now, sugar?"

Sal smiled lavishly.

As Frankie lay down across the unmade bed, she slunk into a stripper pose—hips tilted, head cocked provocatively. Bending down, keeping her movements slow, Sal unclipped her stocking fasteners. With swift movements, she pulled her stockings off, and held them in front of Frankie like she was dangling a gift.

"A striptease, huh? I'm liking this surprise," he said, coal black eyes fixed on Sal's every move.

When she came around the bed he lifted his arms to reach her, and she caught them swiftly. As he strained to kiss her, she danced away from him, pulling his wrists together and pinning them to the wooden rail of the bedstead. Only then did she lean down to press her mouth against his, distracting him as she slipped a stocking through the bars, wrapped it around his wrists, once—"Sal, babe, I didn't know you were into this," he said—twice, and tied it firmly.

Next she moved to the end of the bed. Frankie laughed and she smiled sweetly back at him as she bound his ankles. There was an edge to his laughter, half expectant, half uneasy.

He was pulled taut across the bed.

"I can't move," he said.

"I know."

Sal undid the clasp of her bra and dropped it on the floor. When she started undoing the silk ribbons of her knickers, Frankie licked his lips.

She approached, carrying the fabric scrap of her knickers.

"Now what are you doing?" Frankie asked as she trailed them up from his ankle, over his thigh, brushed over his stiffening cock and lifted them to his face. She let him inhale her scent, and then she tied them over his eyes, using the ribbon to fasten his blindfold tight. She leaned in close.

"Now you can hear me, and feel me, but you can't see me," she whispered.

This time, Frankie didn't laugh. He swallowed.

Over his prone body she draped her hair, pulling it across his skin till it trailed behind her like water. She wrapped his cock in it, brushed it over his balls. He moaned. With slow, hypnotic movements, she swayed back and forth, letting the tips of her long hair drag over him. His cock lay across his belly, long and swollen. A bead of moisture leaked from the head of his glans and wetted the tips of her hair, so that she painted his skin with clear, shining strokes of precum.

Frankie rolled from side to side, lifting his hips up as he begged for more. But Sal kept up her gentle torment, the featherlight stroking of his torso and the wave of her hair over his cock. When his cock started leaping and twitching, she stopped.

Walking silently, barefoot, she slipped away.

In the empty room, Frankie tugged at his bonds, straining to feel the heat of her body against his, murmuring her name.

Moments later, Sal reappeared, and leaned in again to Frankie's ear. She held the kitchen scissors close to his face. *Snip, snip*, she rasped the metal blades against each other. Frankie's body went suddenly rigid, and his mouth fell open.

"Sal?" he asked, turning his head toward the sound and then involuntarily pulling away when he heard her make the cold *snip, snip* noise again. "What's going on—"

"Shhhh…"

She laid her finger on his soft lips and silenced him.

Sal swung herself over his body, straddling him with the scissors still in her hand. She positioned her cunt over his thigh, where she could rub her clit against the fine hairs on his leg. Then she started moving, grinding against his skin, so that he could feel the hot wet fire of her cunt inches from his cock.

As she rocked back and forth, Sal lifted the scissors.

"Sal, what are you doing?" Frankie asked, but she didn't answer.

Her breathing grew faster as she started to cut, lifting handfuls of her hair and shearing them, an inch from her scalp. The cuttings fell over Frankie like leaves from a tree in winter. She knew he could feel the slight weight of her hair piling over his body, tickling and caressing, but not giving any release. She knew he could also feel the kiss of her cunt on his thigh. Her clit was swollen, and chafed against his skin like an axe against flint, showering sparks.

Her orgasm was coming, and this time she wasn't spinning out into the cold blank blissworld. She was somewhere much closer, coming home to herself, her orgasm multiplying, amplifying her body. Frankie's belly and the messed-up bedsheets were covered in the ragged clippings of her hair, and she dropped the scissors as she rode his thigh hard toward an orgasm that he wouldn't share, wouldn't even be able to watch, only hear and feel her as she came down to earth hard, was buried in the sweat and flesh of her body, alive now, lighter, naked and shorn.

When Sal climbed off Frankie, he begged. As she dressed he started to plead, yanking at the twists of nylon that held him fast, raging at the scrap of dirty knickers covering his eyes. Sal's hair covered him like a dry black tide, itching and tormenting him, bringing no relief to his untouched, desperately shining hard-on. Sal rubbed her hand over her head absentmindedly as she looked around for her clothes.

She left him there in his bed strewn with hair, a head full of her black tresses and one single long, curling and treacherous red hair. He could have it all, she thought, walking to the station with her head held high, the spring breeze fresh on the back of her neck. Bare legs, no underwear, cropped hair. He could keep it. For the first time in months, she felt free.

TENILLE BROWN

PULL

FOR ALL NATALIE KNEW, the woman was naked underneath.

She might as well have been, the way her flesh showed through the sheer panty hose: when she bent slightly to pick up her dropped purse, they appeared even more translucent beyond the trim of her skirt.

The lovely stranger might as well have been standing there stark nude, the way Natalie was suddenly warm all over, the way she stopped in her tracks on the sidewalk to watch the woman, and then couldn't remember which direction she was headed.

Natalie decided where she was going wasn't important. What was important was standing close to this woman, so close that the scent of her rosy perfume floated easily up and brushed Natalie's cheeks, kissed her lips and rested inside her nostrils.

And then Natalie bent down to help the woman retrieve the miscellaneous items that had fallen from her pink handbag: a tube of red lipstick, a billfold, a credit card receipt.

Natalie's hand brushed the woman's as she handed them all back to her, and then came the moment, the three-second meeting and locking of their eyes that let Natalie know, yes, it was okay to go a step further, to touch the woman's hand, to maybe ask her name.

Except Natalie found that she couldn't say a word, couldn't do much more than steal one last glance at the woman's nylon-covered legs before she watched the stranger walk away.

Natalie was left to ponder: Was the woman married? Did she have a boyfriend...a *girl*friend? Was she simply not interested?

And as she pondered all these things, the November wind lifted a card from the sidewalk and carried it a few feet before it swirled, turned and landed next to Natalie's feet.

She looked around for spectators, someone who might have been leaning in an apartment window observing, then she bent down and hurriedly scooped it up. Her eyes swallowed the shiny red words. She cleared her throat and shuffled away.

Molly was a nice name. She had looked like a Molly. Natalie recalled how she had stammered over the name like it had six syllables, how she had rambled on like a fool for thirty minutes when what she had to say, what she had wanted to ask, took less than thirty seconds.

And now Natalie waited for a woman named Molly in a dark, crowded café. She waited for the woman named Molly who had strutted down Main Street with shapely thighs and muscular calves. She waited for the woman named Molly who had worn barely there panty hose over her pretty brown legs.

And just as Natalie's shiny, oil-slicked legs began to bounce with impatience, Molly walked in wearing a denim skirt over black mist hose.

Molly shook droplets of rain from her plaid umbrella. She reached up, pulled her fingers through her hair and then straightened her sweater. She smiled when she spotted Natalie.

Her panty hose led the way. If not for the hosiery, Natalie might have given Molly a proper greeting instead of pulling her into a quick embrace before her head dropped and her eyes fixated on the woman's legs.

Then suddenly Molly was speaking.

"I'm sorry?" Natalie leaned in, hoping Molly would believe it was the noise of the crowded café that had caused her to go spontaneously deaf.

"It's wet out there," Molly repeated. Then she pointed toward the door. "You know, outside?"

Natalie nodded. "It wasn't that bad when I got here."

Molly exhaled. "Well, it's a virtual monsoon, now. Ruined my outfit."

"But you look fantastic." The words came out faster than Natalie would have wanted.

Molly cocked her head. "Listen, I'm going to scoot to the toilet and tear off these panty hose. They feel glued to my legs."

Molly tugged at them for emphasis and like soft, threaded magnets, they drew Natalie's eyes to them again. In that instant, she thought about gently touching Molly's hand, telling her it was okay, leave the panty hose in place, but she knew that if the hose remained, her sanity surely would not. So Natalie let Molly get up, her denim skirt heavy with rain, and disappear in the crowd.

When Molly returned, she gave Natalie a quick peck on the cheek.

"Now," Molly said, "what are we drinking?"

But Natalie's mind had turned to other things, like how easily had the hose slid down Molly's legs? Did they smell of her? Were they soft and smooth or coarse and dry? Were they stuffed inside her purse or were they in her pocket?

"You usually hand wash those?" Natalie asked. And sure it was odd. And maybe she could have chosen a better time, but in that moment, the question was as important to her as a proposal of marriage.

"Excuse me?" Confusion was on Molly's face.

"The panty hose," Natalie explained. "I was just remembering how my mom and my sister used to have the things hanging all over the place. I don't get near them myself. They never fit quite right in the um, *crotch* area. But anyway, I was just wondering how you dealt with yours."

Molly's face relaxed a little and she fanned her hand. "Oh, I threw those ones away. I've got tons more."

Natalie nodded and tried to pay attention to the outpouring of words that came next, but she couldn't sit still, couldn't concentrate, and when Molly asked a question, Natalie couldn't respond.

"Excuse me," Natalie said, finally. "Restroom."

Molly nodded her acknowledgment and waved the bartender over.

Natalie slipped through the crowd and pushed through the bathroom door looking for the trash can. And right there on top, she found what she so desperately sought.

Natalie waited for an older woman to wash and dry her hands and walk out, before she grabbed the crumpled wad of panty hose and stuffed them in her jacket pocket. She smiled, satisfied, and returned to the bar.

Molly's back was turned, and she was sipping Amaretto. She turned and winked when Natalie took her seat beside her. And with Molly's warm, damp hose safely tucked inside her jacket pocket, Natalie felt able to look the woman in the face, to notice her hair and soft hazel eyes.

She felt able to reach out, to put her hands on Molly's knee and ask, "So, Molly, what is it that you do?"

Natalie didn't consider herself a betting gal, except that three out of three times that she and Molly had gotten together, Molly had covered her shapely chestnut legs in panty hose.

If Natalie had made the wager tonight, she would have won, if only on a technicality, as Molly sat three feet away from her in the passenger's seat, the bottom half of her sporting a striped pleated skirt and red fishnet stockings with garters. She held a cigarette between her fingers.

They were in Natalie's car, having just enjoyed dinner and drinks. They had talked until they were tired and now the only sound left to be heard was Lenny Kravitz belting out an electric love song.

Maybe it was the music. Maybe it was the moist night air. Maybe it was the smell of Molly's menthol cigarette mingling with her perfume that made Natalie lean over and kiss her cheek.

Natalie couldn't be sure if it was Molly's lips, her soft hands or smooth thighs that made her take the cigarette form Molly's hand and put it out. Then she kissed Molly's lips, slipping her tongue inside Molly's mouth.

Molly welcomed the kiss. Her small hands rose up and gently gripped Natalie's head. She pushed her fingers through the tiny, coarse curls that covered Natalie's scalp.

Their tongues touched and swirled. Their bodies became impatient. Natalie's hands traveled over Molly's thin blouse, caressing her taut breasts. Her hands slipped down to Molly's waist, squeezing her hips, gliding across her ass.

Molly wanted more. She led Natalie to the backseat where they stretched their bodies along the cool leather. Natalie positioned herself between Molly's legs. Molly lifted her feet and tossed them across Natalie's shoulders, the sharp, silver heel of her shoe pressing against the glass.

Molly lifted her hips so that Natalie could gather her skirt and bring it up over her hips. Natalie lowered her head between Molly's thighs. The silky smoothness of stockings brushed against her cheeks. She planted quick, hot kisses on Molly's cunt.

Molly's wetness seeped through her panties, moistening the lace crotch. She held her thighs firmly on either side of Natalie's face.

Pulling back, Natalie removed Molly's panties and laid them aside. Her lips again met the warm space between Molly's legs. She placed gentle kisses on the delicate peak that stood between the folds of her cunt. Natalie kissed Molly there, her tongue traveling slowly in and out, her fingers grasping and reaching to find places her tongue could not.

Molly's sex oozed warmth. She wet Natalie's lips and chin as she pushed against Natalie's mouth, lifting her ass from the leather seat. The she reached down and held the back of Natalie's head, brought her face forward so that her mouth pressed harder against her cunt. Molly shivered. And she squirmed. She came in sharp spasms against Natalie's mouth.

Leaning down, Natalie kissed Molly on her stocking-covered thigh before she laid her head there and breathed.

Molly had grown comfortable in Natalie's apartment, knew her way around the kitchen, had even claimed a small corner of the closet. She reclined on the couch now, her legs stretched across Natalie's lap while she sipped a beer. She had stripped down to a T-shirt and panty hose.

"I'm cold," Molly said. "You got some pants or something I could slip on?" She nudged Natalie with her elbow.

Natalie twisted her lips. "Check the drawers."

Molly planted a cool, wet kiss on Natalie's nose and disappeared into the bedroom.

Natalie had gazed at the television screen for fifteen minutes before her body stiffened and she stood up, fear rising up within her.

Natalie called out, "Molly, you okay in there?"

The silence stung her ears.

Anxious feet carried Natalie into the bedroom where she found Molly on the floor, surrounded by mounds of satin and silk, fishnet and nylon. Molly glared at the pile of stockings and panty hose, then she looked up at Natalie.

"What the hell *are* these?" Horror showed on Molly's face.

Natalie struggled to find the words. "They're…well, um…"

"They're not yours, right? You don't even wear them, right? Are you some kind of freak or something?" Molly tossed pair after pair aside. "Look! I threw these away. And these are run in three places. And these… Damn it, Natalie, these aren't even *mine*!"

Molly pushed the pile of stockings aside and scrambled to her feet. She pushed Natalie aside, grabbed her clothes, and headed toward the front door. Natalie, close on Molly's heels, made it there just as Molly pulled the door open.

"Wait," Natalie breathed, desperation in her eyes.

The words caught up in her throat, dried up on her lips, clung to the air like mist.

"What, Natalie? What do you have to say?" Her lips puckered in a pout.

Natalie breathed. She reached for Molly, held her by the waist until Molly brushed her hands away. Natalie's hand brushed Molly's nylon-covered thigh. Her fingers found the waistband of her panty hose.

Natalie tugged, tucking her fingers inside.

"What the hell are you *doing*?" Molly's voice was a squeal.

Natalie pulled. The hose ripped.

"You're *crazy*!" Her voice was softer now, almost transparent.

And Natalie continued. She tugged and pulled until she held a handful of sheer nylon.

Molly shook her head and slipped through the door, bare legs carrying her to her car.

And Natalie let Molly go, satisfied in knowing that she now had the best part, the sweetest part of her, tucked safely inside her palm.

BARBARA PIZIO

FANCY PANTS

FIONA'S DRESSER DRAWERS are overflowing with sexy undergarments: lacy little thongs, silk string bikinis and soft cotton panties. I love how smooth and shapely her ass looks in tight pants when she's wearing a thong. And she's always adorable lounging about on Sunday morning in her floral-print cotton panties. But I must confess that my personal favorite is a pair of black mesh boy-cut briefs with three horizontal lines of tiny pink ruffles that adorn her best feature—her ass.

Fiona's lush cheeks peek out of the bottom of those short-shorts in the sexiest way. They're a fleshy tease just waiting to be slapped. I could spank her for hours, content to watch her soft flesh jiggle and jump each time my hand connects with her bottom.

Early in our relationship, Fiona let me know how much she enjoys being put over someone's knee. I had never spanked a woman before, but I had never met a woman like Fiona, either. She is as kinky as hell and wildly vocal in bed, often letting me know exactly what she wants and how she wants it. More than once, her moans of longing and shouts of ecstasy have pushed me over the edge. While I've had many happy opportunities to tie her up, blindfold her and even fuck her in public, I've noticed that nothing makes her pussy drip more than being spanked. Fiona owns all sorts of paddles, crops and toys, and I've enjoyed trying them all out on her naughty little bottom, but I prefer using my bare hand. Our sex is always spectacular after I've spanked her, and I never pass up the opportunity to turn her ass-cheeks red.

Last weekend was one such occasion. We had a date set for Saturday night, and I showed up a little too early at her apartment. When Fiona answered the door, she was wearing black high heels, a sheer black tank top and those delicious black briefs. As soon as I saw her in that outfit I knew our reservation would go unused.

"I'm almost ready," Fiona promised, brushing her long dark hair away from her face. "I just need to slip into my dress." Then she ran off into her bedroom. As she sprinted across the living room, her breasts danced inside her tank top, her tiny pink nipples nearly poking through the see-through fabric. Her ruffled fanny bounced behind her and the sight of her creamy cheeks hanging out of those panties sent a jolt of electricity straight to my cock.

I quickly followed her into the bedroom. She was about to step into her dress when she turned, saw me standing there and flashed me a smile. "Just give me a sec," she started saying.

"Don't bother," I told her. Fiona tilted her head and gave me a questioning look. I came up behind her, wrapped my arms around her and starting kissing her slender neck. She gave a contented sigh and I felt her melt in my arms. I brought one hand up under her tank top and caressed her breast, pinching her nipple until she gasped. She instantly pushed back against me, wriggling her bottom against my hardening cock. While I continued to toy with her nipple, I trailed my other hand down her tanned stomach and over her fabric-covered mound. She moaned and turned to kiss me. I palmed her crotch as I slipped my tongue into her hot mouth. Her lips were slippery with gloss and I kissed her until its slick wetness was gone, our tongues wrestling in desperate passion. I cupped her pussy and could sense her growing moisture. She ground down against my hand ever so slightly, trying to increase the pressure of my touch.

"Not so fast," I gently chastised, and felt her shudder in my embrace. I bent her forward and placed her hands on the mattress in front of her. I began rubbing my palm over her ruffled bottom and she groaned out loud, knowing what was coming. Slowly, I ran my fingers up and down her bare thighs and then cupped each of her plush cheeks, making her wait as long as I could possibly stand. She was wiggling her bottom impatiently when I raised my hand and brought it down firmly on her ass. She gasped loudly and thrust back at me, longing for more. Her panties were so sheer that I could see my handprint rise to the surface of her skin with that single slap. I continued spanking her as she swayed her bottom enticingly, urging me on.

The first few slaps were greeted with groans of longing. I landed a flurry of swats all over the entirety of her ass, making it blush prettily. Then I turned my attention to the lower part of her cheeks, the part that peeks out of those panties so invitingly. The contact of bare flesh with bare flesh made a sharp report. I placed one hand on the small of her back and began spanking each cheek slowly at first, alternating from one to the other, and then began picking up the pace. With the addition of another dozen hard, sharp slaps her bottom blossomed from a delicate pink to a rosy red. Her groans had turned into little sharp squeaks and her whole body shook each time my hand connected with her ass. When she began shifting her weight from one foot to the other, I knew she'd had enough for the moment.

I turned her around and sat her on the bed. Fiona winced slightly when her bottom hit the cool sheets. Her breasts heaved as she took deep breaths, her hair fell tousled around her face in sexy disarray. I knelt before her and dove between her spread thighs. Her cunt was positively soaked. She fell back on the bed and moaned with delight as I mouthed her cunt through the mesh. My senses were nearly over-whelmed by her musky scent. Her fragrant juices had seeped through the fabric and I lapped her panty-covered slit, eager to drink up as much as I could. I slipped my hands inside the bottom of her briefs and grasped her well-spanked cheeks, bringing her cunt even closer to my mouth. Her asscheeks felt hot in my hands and she squealed when I squeezed them roughly.

Her clit was puffy and swollen underneath the panties and I con-centrated all of my efforts on it as she bucked her hips and thrust her pussy up toward my face. I knew that tonguing her through her panties like that would draw out her orgasm for a torturously long time. I continued lapping at her while she whimpered and cried, begging me to take off her panties. Soon her pleas stopped, but her bucking and sighing didn't. I lapped and sucked on her clit until she started shaking and crying out, "Oh, oh, oh!" Her whole body trembled and her hands clutched at the back of my head. I felt her pussy twitch against my lips and tongue as her juice flooded my mouth.

Now I was the one who was desperate. I yanked down her juice-slick panties. My dick was ready to burst; I had to fuck her. "On your hands and knees," I ordered breathlessly. Her face was flushed and she was still panting from her orgasm, but she quickly obeyed. Her ass was beautifully pink and I couldn't wait to spank her again while I fucked her from behind.

Fiona's cunt was so incredibly slick that I slammed my cock into her with no resistance. I fucked her hard and fast, pausing every few thrusts to spank her bottom. Each time my hand connected with her bare ass, her cunt tightened around my cockhead. She cried out with each slap and thrust her ass back toward me, wanting more of everything. I grasped her hips in my hands and began pulling her down hard on me, loving the feel of her warm cheeks meeting my thighs. Her juice dripped down my tightening balls as I pounded into her frantically. Fiona was moaning loudly and urging me to fuck her. I was already fucking her as hard as I could, but hearing her beg me like that was almost enough to make me come all by itself. Soon she started whimpering the way she does when she's close to orgasm. When she cried out and I felt her pussy flutter around my thrusting shaft, I totally lost it. I let loose with a loud groan and pumped her full of cream.

The two of us collapsed onto the bed, and I hugged her tightly to me, both of us panting and barely able to speak. I could still feel the heat emanating from her ass as she snuggled up against me, and my hand was still stinging.

Those seven o'clock reservations were long gone, but neither of us minded one bit that we'd be eating in that night.

KRISTINA LLOYD

BOOT CAMP

IVE INMATES ARE SITTING ON THE LAWN on wooden chairs, as nice as can be. It's sunny here, with shadows of skinny trees slanting across the grass and light burnishing the five pairs of army boots arrayed before me. Our counselor is wearing tennis shoes. It makes me suspicious. Punishment shouldn't feel this good.

I've been waiting awhile and my knees are starting to ache. I'm on all fours at the head of a horseshoe of feet. I know when they let me move, my knees will be red raw, cross-hatched with imprinted grass. Lots of little blades. I should have worn a longer dress. Or knee pads. Hell, I should've been born wearing knee pads.

Lee has the biggest boots and I can tell he's lived a full life already. Maybe he's seen active service. Maybe he's been talking about war for the last fifteen minutes and maybe I'm meant to be listening. But I'm not. Instead I'm counting the eyelets of his boots, over and over. It's the only way to stay sane. Three pairs of eyelets rising up to the metal loops of a speed-lacing system, black laces crisscrossing over leather tongues, as beautiful as corsetry. They are British Army assault boots, size 12, standard issue for Soldier 95. I know this without asking.

José, the pussy, is wearing German jump boots. The leather is extra supple, the ankles have padded collars, and there's no need to break them in. Before I realized this, I once tried hitting on a guy by admiring his jumps, and he said, "Yeah, they're awesome. Fit like a glove right away." I couldn't see the point after that. I'm not looking for Cinderella.

Lee had to break his boots in. His feet would have ached, skin chafing and blistering, open sores stuck with fuzzy bits of sock, wounds painted with liquid skin. Maybe he stuck moleskin on the hot spots, tried saltwater to toughen up his toes. Either way, he had to seduce his boots into submission. And he had to suffer to get there. Oh yes, sir, Lee earned those beauties, and for his pain and his patience, I would happily lick his molded, dual-density polyurethane soles.

I had them all to myself last night, the left foot and the right. Alone with Mr. Moon, I pulled out the laces, got rid of the dirt in each tongue and stripped off the paint. I lit a candle and kneeled over them, warming a spoon of polish over the flame, a spitshine junkie at her army boot shrine. I gave them four good layers of polish and let them dry several hours. And here they are now, back on his feet, dulled and black, waiting for my magic.

"Spitshine," says our soft-voiced counselor because today that's the name I asked for. "What is it you want to do here?"

I'm so wet and loose. He knows exactly what I want to do. *Exactly* because I wrote him a twelve-thousand-word essay and he graded it Bminus. "The structure was a little off, Kelly, and you didn't come to any conclusions."

"You dumb fuck," I thought as he handed back the paper. "There *are* no conclusions. This is it. Don't you get it? There *is* no end in sight."

So here I am on my hands and knees, gazing at five pairs of army boots, all in need of some love and attention. I'm so horny I can barely kneel. The detention block's at the far end of the lawn, and every Tom, Dick and Harry in there has probably got binoculars on my butt. The guys, *my* guys, sit with their feet planted wide, pants tucked in or hitched up so I can see everything there is to see; every last eyelet and lolling tongue; every stitch, scuff and scratch; every line of dust and each grain of Iraqi sand lodged in the creases that are etched in the leather.

That's how it feels. It's hallucinogenically intense down here. It's the Van Gogh painting five times over. And I'm at the head of this horseshoe of booted feet, and next to me on the grass is my Tupperware box of kit—polishes, wax, a range of brushes, picks, water bottle, panty hose, old T-shirts cut into rags—and Mr. Larry H. Condell is asking what I want?

Well, what the fuck do you think I want, Condi? The last waltz?

The setup's almost too much. Five guys baring their boots, and it's all for me. Sure, they've got their problems too, but this week it's my turn. We're engaged in some kind of cooperative rehab therapy. We learn about our own problems through learning about each other's. It's meant to be helpful. And it is, totally. I've learned for example, that Lee's problem is he can't stop thinking about pussy. He wants to eat it, touch it, taste it, lick it, smell it.

In our first group session he sat there, hands held in his lap, staring at the floor as we waited for him to speak. He's huge, well over six feet, shoulders wide as a door. Eventually he closed his eyes, knuckles turning white, clenching like a prayer as he confessed to the room. I watched as the words came out, saw the blush creep over his face, the slight quiver of his nostrils. His voice was sad and shameful, barely above a whisper, and he said, "I live and I breathe pussy."

I tell you, that is so helpful it's keeping me awake at nights.

But now it's my turn. Having to say it is so humiliating. My throat nearly seizes up and I don't know if I can. But I stare at Lee's feet, blades of grass fringing his thick soles, and every inch of my skin prickles with need. There is something much bigger than me and it forces me to speak. "Sir," I say quietly. "I want to polish these boots till I can see my reflection."

"Louder!" barks Steve, shuffling in his seat.

Steve wears French combats, size 9. They're classic and simple: six pairs of eyelets and a broad ankle cuff fastened by two black side-buckles. Bright sunlight rests like a small, still star on the topmost buckle. I can't look up from them, I really can't. But I can picture his face. He's got these dark gypsy eyes that try to draw you into his world, and thick sultry lips. He's small and intense, looks a little sad at times but you can tell underneath he's crazy. Too much shit in his head. It's written all over him. He's very fuckable, and he knows it, but that's never been a problem for me.

However, he isn't wearing British Army assault boots, Soldier 95, and Lee is.

"Sir," I repeat in a strong voice. "I want to polish these boots till I can see my reflection."

They've heard me loud and clear. No one speaks. We all stay in silence, my voice echoing in our seven baffled brains. All of them are looking at me and I'm looking at them; or more specifically, at their feet. I don't know what to do. I don't know if I'm supposed to, you know, expand on my desire. Maybe some bull about how ashamed I am? Condi's always doing this, saying nothing till it gets so awkward someone cracks and breaks the silence.

But I don't say anything, nor does anyone else, and I wait and wait until eventually Condi says, very kindly, "Spitshine, you don't need my permission to do that."

This isn't very professional of him. He shouldn't be the first to speak but I figure he's bored or hard, and he wants some action. But it was the wrong thing to say and now I'm totally paralyzed. Permission? He thinks I lack the ability to act without permission? Jeez, I don't think he even *read* my essay, did he? I've been taking permission since I was fourteen years old, grabbing it by the neck and just damn well taking it. Hell, it's that kind of behavior that gets you locked up in the first place.

I'd heard rumors about what goes on in here. On the outside they call it the Pervs' Penitentiary though officially it's the Correctional Rehabilitation Academy for Venereal Extremists (CRAVE). They believe in aversion therapy, just like my dad did when he caught me stealing one of his cigarettes. He took me out into the yard and made me smoke till I was sick.

I will never get sick of army boots. I will never tire of polishing them. But now I can't act because Condi, with his dumb-ass reverse psychology, has effectively given me his permission, and it's making me feel nauseous.

So once again we're steeped in the silence I'm getting used to: the troubled silence of a bunch of alienated, incarcerated deviants, freaks and paraphiliacs, all of us with hope in our hearts. It's powerful stuff.

We're only in here because we ran into a little bad luck. Me? They caught me heisting boots from a military surplus store. I ought to have stayed home, working on my smile, but I got the urge for more. I was careless, and got busted. And they thought that gave them the right to shine a torch into my soul. I remember a time when people used to have civil liberties. Not that long ago, either. Lee? Jeez, I dread to think what they caught him doing.

After a while, I glance up and catch his eye. I see his Adam's apple bob in his throat and I have to look away. Lee is so beautiful. His hair is velvet-short and though he's big and strong, there's a kind of fraught melancholy to him. His brow has a permanent low-grade pucker, and he wears an expression of someone forever on the verge of getting hurt.

It's because he's always thinking about pussy.

I look at his boots, wanting to slide my tongue into creases he's created with years of walking, marching, running, living. A bee buzzes nearby, growing loud and soft before fading to nothing. The sun beats down and I can smell baked earth and grass. It's lucky my wrists are strong because this position could take its toll. Beneath my dress, my back is slicked with sweat. I see a twitch in the material of Lee's camouflage pants. His hands have been resting obediently on his thighs, and I guess he felt the need for a readjustment. Wow. Just…wow.

In the silence, I hear him swallow. My groin is thickening and every breath I draw seems to last forever.

Then Lee says, "Polish my boots, Spitshine." His voice is cool and steady, though a little uncertain. "Crawl at my feet and polish my boots." It's growing in confidence now and making me hot, all the hairs standing up on the back of my neck. "Polish my boots, Spitshine, until you can see your reflection. Until...until they're shining like black mirrors. Until the toes are like glass, so bright, so...so fucking bright that I could see your pussy in 'em." There is a silence. "Shit. I'm sorry, Kel. I'm real sorry."

There's no need for him to be sorry because I'm right there at his feet, trying not to overbreathe. I unlace his boots. This guy's going nowhere. I've got my kit with me and from it I unfold my crumpled, polish-smeared sheet of instructions and lay it on the grass, held down with a couple of brushes. I know these instructions off by heart but that's not the point. I still need to read them, still need to have those sentences telling me what to do. Like right now, I'm buffing with my horsehair brush and those instructions are whispering to me: *Abuse it. Work it hard.*

It's like a voice inside my head. Oh, and I abuse it and I work it till the boots are shining nicely. But it's not the shine I want. The shine I want is a spitshine, and a spitshine takes time.

My hands are trembling as I pour water into a little bowl. The sound is so refreshing. I'm in the kind of mood where I could dip my head to it and lap like a pretty kitty but I don't want to risk confusing the guys with cross-kinks.

And the instructions say to me: *Wet a section of the cloth and wring it out. You want it damp but not dripping wet.*

I twist the cloth and droplets tinkle into the bowl. Lee's legs are solid, and his camouflage-clad shins don't move an inch. His boots

— 43 —

gleam, and the leather ripples around his ankles like fabric petrified mid-fall. I glance up. In his BDU pants and tight white vest, he's a statue of flesh, bronzed shoulders practically rigid as he breathes long and low, gazing down as I kneel at his feet. He doesn't look at me. He looks past me, staring at a patch of grass. But I know what he's thinking about. We *all* know what he's thinking about, day and night, night and day.

I edge into a good position and flip the lid on the tin of polish, inhaling that dirty chemical smell. I wrap the damp cloth around my first two fingers, gripping it to make a nice taut surface, and I read my instructions. *Dab a SMALL amount of polish on the cloth.*

Done. Sir.

Begin lightly stroking the surface of the leather in small circles, working a section at a time. Small circles, over and over. Small little circles.

This is the part that makes me spin, and all my spitshine dreams are being realized. I cup Lee's heel and start rubbing at the back, small little circles, just like the voice tells me. The polish streaks at first then it starts to smooth out, the shine rising. I do those circles over and over, more and more lightly, and the gloss starts to come. I dip my finger in the water, pinch the cloth, take a dab of polish and on and on I go, making my beautiful little circles.

It takes a long old time. Leather is skin. The polish layers have to be molecular, next to nothing, and you have to work and work, keeping it so gentle. There are no shortcuts here, no quick routes to brilliance.

When I spitshine, I swear it's like I'm becoming the boots. It's calming and sexy, and I slip into a kind of trance. I'd like to describe it as "spiritual" but I'm turned on and that seems awfully blasphemous.

— 44 —

It's tough to explain. Okay, let me try. It's sort of a hot, horny, meditative vibe where I'm zoned out and tuned in simultaneously; and all the arousal I ever knew is resting in my groin and a river's running through me, so slow and so warm, and my clit is beating like a little heart, like new life, and my lust is spread across the starry starry night, thin as my layers of Parade Gloss; and no one can reach me and I'm ravenous, and that little beating heart is right at the center of the entire fucking universe.

Yeah, that's about how it feels.

By the time I'm working on the toes, I am God. And God has a very swollen clitoris.

Finally, my face appears, distorted and shrunk in the toes of Lee's boots. It stares back at me twice, like this is some tiny hall of mirrors, and I know I'm nearly done here. It's taken over an hour and that high polish is so sharp I could come.

Tomorrow, I'll work on Steve's combats. The day after, Louis's jungle boots, then José's jumps and Bobby's tankers.

If you ask me, I'd say aversion therapy is no way to cure a fetishist, especially when the counselors don't bother dishing up the bad shit with the good. You know, like electrodes to go with your psychic over-investment in panties? I swear, this institution would've been closed down years ago if it weren't sanctioned by a bunch of deviants who get off on administering phony treatments.

But I warm to the whole deal later that evening when I'm queuing in the mess hall for dinner. The place is a freak show of people in rubber, latex, fur and feathers, diapers, body harnesses and white surgical coats. Some folk have a hunted look. They haven't realized what a blast it is in here. Others who know better carry a certain glow, like cats that got the cream.

I notice his boots first, the brightest blackest things in the hall. They look liquid, as if they're made of ink. I can't look him in the eye. He sidles in behind me with his tray, an irregular GI Joe. He doesn't say a word and I don't turn around. I can sense him. I can feel the presence of his big solid body. Then he bends close, his breath tickling my ear, and in a voice full of shyness and secrets, he says, "Kelly, I want to spitshine your pussy."

And I melt. I just melt.

And I gaze at his boots, figuring I ought to offer him a little therapy because Lee and I, we understand each other, and together we're gonna let it shine.

JEREMY EDWARDS

SLIGHTLY AJAR

FIRST, SHE STARTED TO LEAVE the door slightly ajar. More or less closed—but not, technically, shut. Open just enough so that the merry reverberations of her waterfall would squeeze through the crack, creating a subtle soundtrack to accompany the glowing sliver of bathroom fluorescence that I could see from across the dimly lit bedroom.

On the first couple of occasions, I attributed it to carelessness. I assumed that Bernadette had intended to shut the door but hadn't pushed hard enough. But soon a pattern emerged. The narrow stripe of light became a reliable indication that Bernadette was in there peeing. This was the only time the door was slightly ajar, neither really open nor really closed. It was what a statistician would call a one-to-one correlation, and a mathematician an "if and only if" statement. If Bernadette was in there peeing, the door was ajar; if the door was ajar, Bernadette was in there peeing. It was a logically airtight correspondence.

It excited me.

I didn't know why it excited me to have two inches of bathroom light bring me closer to my own wife's tinkling, but it did. This was a woman I'd fucked almost every night for three years, whose most intimate areas I'd probed and explored and titillated and feasted upon till I knew every one of her erogenous hot spots better than I knew the back of my own cock. And yet it triggered a novel sort of arousal to hear her peeing with the door slightly ajar.

I became accustomed to this curious new habit of hers, and I waited to see what, if anything, would develop from it.

Was something expected of me?

A few weeks after she had introduced the sliver of bathroom light into our relationship, she began talking to me through the crack. Now, we have a little rule between us that we try not to talk when we can't see each other's faces. We both grew up in homes where family members would shout to each other from the bottom of the stairs, from far corners of the house, or even from outdoors, through the screen windows…and we were determined to be more civilized than that. We'd learned early on how easy it was to mishear content or misconstrue tone in the absence of visual cues. So our rule is that if I have something to say and Bernadette is not in sight, then I will go find her, and vice versa.

Therefore, Bernadette had to know that if she spoke to me from her womanly perch on the toilet when the door was almost-but-not-quite shut, I would instinctively come into the bathroom, so as to better facilitate effective communication. After all, *she* clearly wasn't going anywhere for the time being—so the burden would be on me to come to her.

The first time it happened, this instinct propelled me into the bathroom before I was fully conscious of the implications. But when I gazed on the sight of my wife, poised elegantly on the commode, her panties rolled slightly out of place—aptly analogous to the barely ajar door I'd opened—it hit me that I'd walked into a hitherto-unknown space. I felt as if I'd entered a shrine. Though I was, of course, entirely familiar with our bathroom, it had become at this moment a sacred locus of feminine mystery: the place where a woman urinates.

She was asking if there were any mushrooms left. I'd made a stew the night before, and she wondered if I'd used them all up. It was a reasonable thing to ask at 6:00 p.m., with dinner on our minds. But did she really need to know the answer before returning from her brief visit to the bathroom?

As I stared at her bare thighs, which emerged with a jaunty raunchiness from her bunched-up skirt, I became conscious of my erection. And of the fact that I couldn't, for the life of me, recall the status of the mushrooms.

Though Bernadette had actually concluded her pissing before I'd arrived, she didn't appear to be in a hurry to remove her bare ass from the seat. So we stayed where we were, while I muttered something about checking the refrigerator. I noticed that her smile seemed to have a special glow to it.

Finally, she reached behind and under herself to wipe her pussy dry, thus exposing me to a routine gesture of feminine maintenance—

one that I naturally knew about, but had never before observed. She did it with such a graceful motion that it was anything but mundane. And it surprised me that she did it from behind, which somehow made it sexier. I felt a vibration in my groin that had an odd, sentimental quality to it. For some reason, this act of hygiene emphasized my wife's softness and put a tender finish on my libido. I reached for the vanity to steady myself.

When we made love later that night, I was thinking about what I'd seen before dinner.

Over time, the crack in the door began to widen. And the unnecessary conversations that Bernadette engineered became a frequent feature of her evening tinkles. These dialogues were always timed so that I'd enter her sanctuary shortly after her activity had trickled to a conclusion, but before she had wiped. I didn't fully understand her motivation, but I knew that the ritual was one that always left me tingling, and Bernadette glowing. And it gradually dawned on me that this, of course, *was* the motivation.

The timing of Bernadette's toilet-seat conversations changed momentously one evening. "Are you going to be able to drive me to work tomorrow?" she inquired. In this instance, she spoke just moments after she'd dashed out of sight. I had returned home only a few minutes earlier, and had found her waiting for me in the bedroom, but evidently ready to head into the bathroom without further ado. I'd noticed that she was already undoing the belt buckle at the waist of her denim skirt as she crossed the threshold.

Upon hearing her voice from beyond the unclosed door, I looked at the wide shaft of light as if it were a beacon of joy.

I entered.

She had not only dropped her denim skirt and powder blue panties; she had allowed her feet to step out of them entirely. Her legs were spread generously as she prepared to let go. From her navel on down, I could see everything.

She sat poised, exposed in naked glory. And here, as in the bedroom, she had waited for me. Not a drop had yet emerged to kiss her quivering pussy and journey down into the bowl.

I started to stammer something about tomorrow's car pool, when an impressive roar overtook me. How could I never have ventured in to watch before? How could I have missed such a wonderful, erotic phenomenon? Smooth thighs, sensuous bush, adorable nether lips…frame and backdrop for one of nature's most breathtaking miracles—a woman peeing. A woman spreading her legs and giving in to an insistent private fountainhead. Letting all her senses be overtaken by the aquatic bliss of the flow, and allowing—in effect requesting— that I watch every drop come out of her.

I was enchanted by the fact that it was difficult to see through the rapids to discern the actual source. I was fascinated by the illusion that the water was coming from everywhere at once. It was spectacular.

Bernadette, in her present guise as a urinating woman, seemed to exude a sexuality more potent than anything I'd previously seen her express. This simple biological process, in its feminine incarnation, threw her femaleness into such sharp relief, both anatomically and sensually, that I felt this might be the quintessential context in which to admire her. Bernadette, legs apart, immersed in this all-absorbing task, was perhaps the most beautiful Bernadette I'd ever seen.

Idiotically, I still felt obligated to address the question about who was driving whom to work the next day. I struggled to concentrate, despite the fact that I had my hand in my underwear, stroking hard. "I have to be in the office a little early, so…"

She interrupted at once. "Shh! Please, Derek. Shut up, honey. Shut up and watch me," she said rapidly. Her face was transfixed, watching me watch her. She attempted to spread her legs even further. It was physically impossible…but she tried, with a symbolic compulsiveness. Her cheeks were flushed and her eyes were half-closed, though still focused on me. She was now squirming, clearly making the most of her intimate sensations. Then she started to laugh—a strange mixture of delight and release. "You're watching…" She was as turned on as I'd ever seen her.

She grabbed herself. Her eyes closed as she cried my name.

She was still pissing forcefully across her fingers as the orgasm cooked through her. I imagined how the warm waters must feel against her hand. This was when I shot my seed all over her thighs.

Testing the Waters

He didn't know it, but my obsession had begun the night our friends Tammy and Craig came over to sample beers. It was around midnight when they left, and—for the umpteenth time on this lager-laden evening—I had to piss for all I was worth. I ran upstairs, not even waiting till I was in the bathroom to start sliding my panties down. Just as I closed the door behind me, I heard Derek's footsteps on the stairs. By the time I'd settled into place, I knew he was in the bedroom.

The water came out of me quickly at first, then slowly and deliciously. And I realized, as all my muscles relaxed with the joy of peeing, that I was seriously horny. After three years of marriage, it was suddenly driving me wild to know that Derek was on the other side of the bathroom door while I sat here, exposed and tingling.

I'd had quasi-orgasmic peeing sessions many times in the past, but they'd always existed in isolation. It had never occurred to me to link them to my sex life with Derek. But now I found myself craving something I'd never craved before—that Derek could be in here watching me…dipping his hand into my water, touching my nakedness and feeling my two wetnesses.

It struck me that with my legs spread immodestly and my pee flowing freely, I was uninhibited, open, and sensually awake on a level that rivaled or perhaps even surpassed the sharing of myself that occurred during sex. My entire body seemed united in the electric carnality of what was happening between my legs. I felt like I wanted to piss forever. And I suddenly had a revelation that, as a sexual being, this was perhaps the ultimate, essential me—the horny, natural woman with water flowing out of her feminine juncture, whose intimate muscles and nerves were dancing euphorically around her stream. And it struck me that this was the woman I now desperately wanted Derek to meet.

I dragged it out as long as I could, until I simply couldn't pee anymore. While the warm, lingering drops still tickled my most sensuous zone, I brought myself off, trembling on the toilet seat with my panties at my ankles. I could hear Derek puttering around in the next room as I came.

That night in bed, I pounced on Derek even more enthusiastically than usual. As my cunt pulsated around him, I caught myself fantasizing that I was pissing in his presence.

I knew I had to test the waters. So I started "forgetting" to close the door all the way. I began chattering to him from the toilet, so he'd come into the bathroom just after I'd finished, when I was still cunt-naked on the seat. It made me slippery to play host to him while I sat there.

Then, it was time to take the next step.

I was wearing a short denim skirt that evening, I remember. I felt the slow, lazy beginnings of a need about thirty minutes before he was due to arrive home. Once I'd made the decision to wait for him, it became a pleasant challenge. I turned it into an autoerotic game, nurturing my kinky predilection for the thrill of "holding it"—something it was high time I told Derek about, I realized. (Would he get off on it?) I turned a reverent focus to the current dammed up inside me, and I paced myself through the passing minutes of anticipation and excitement. The need blossomed, and at moments I felt like I was about to lose it, to wet myself wildly over the bedroom floor—and it further aroused me to fantasize about Derek finding me in such a situation. But then I'd recross my legs or wedge a hand into my crotch…and immediately the impending flood would become tame again, a force that I could control a while longer and whose pulsing tingle I could continue to revel in lewdly. Like a skillful woman on the brink of an intense orgasm, who prolongs that moment for as long as she can continue to milk her pleasure from the tension, I was as reluctant to release as I was certain that the release would rock me to the heels when I finally permitted it. Every minute, half of me hoped that Derek was about to pull up in the driveway and accompany me to the commode for my cascade. But the other half hoped his arrival would be delayed just a few minutes longer, so I could keep squeezing my thighs and playing with that inner tickle.

He arrived at last, and I lured him into the bathroom by dint of some inane conversation. I roared forth with a piss so glorious that it made some of orgasm's greatest hits pale in comparison. And Derek saw every fluid ounce of it. I was in fucking paradise, sprawling there on the toilet for him. He was very cute, trying to answer my irrelevant question about the car while I showed him what it looks and feels like for a self-actualized lady to piss herself giddy after deliberately playing into thirty minutes of overtime.

It Never Rains But It Pours

After that night, my wife's routine need to urinate gained the status of a featured attraction in our life. Our evenings now often seemed to be structured around Bernadette pissing her heart out while I watched, crouching on the tile floor. She would finger herself, sometimes not even waiting till her stream abated. I would jerk off, usually coming while she was still in full flow. Sometimes it was my hand that caressed her wet pussy, instead of her own. Whatever the details, the sense of intimacy was indescribable.

It had always been common for me to look at Bernadette and think, "She's so very beautiful." These days, this thought was no less common; but it was often followed by the kinky corollary, "Will she have to pee soon?" I might have been troubled by this obsession, were it not for my confidence that Bernadette approved of it, and indeed had deliberately encouraged it. And I was not left alone to wonder when her panties would be coming down. For Bernadette had begun to keep me informed, with blushes and whispers, whenever she felt the liquid tickling up inside her.

When we had wine with dinner, I would watch her as she drank— study her face, her posture. "Is she starting to feel the need yet?" I would wonder. With every ambiguous shift in her position, with every swallow she took from her wine goblet or her water glass, I would anticipate the inevitable. And on the nights on which she opened a beer, I could barely contain myself as I envisioned the fluid consequences.

Imagine that you happened upon the banks of the Niagara River, and that the falls had been magically switched off. And imagine that you never knew that there were supposed to be falls there. You would, I believe, still find it gorgeous. But if you knew about the falls, you'd miss them. At times, now, this was how I felt about my wife's pussy. It was as lovely as it had ever been. But, at certain moments, what I craved most was to see it with her water pouring out of it.

It was when we were dining downtown with Tammy and Craig one Saturday that I realized how absolutely fixated I'd become on Bernadette's waterworks. We were indulging liberally in a selection of marvelous wines—with plenty of lemon-tinged water to accompany them—and I kept wondering when Bernadette would need to excuse herself. My attention wandered, again and again, to her body language—did I detect a pressure, a shifting of weight? I would be heading for the restroom myself before too long, and I was speculating that the rather pleasant sensations I was feeling behind my zipper were analogous to what she was feeling in her panties. As I communed with the familiar presence of my own beckoning reservoir—relishing that mixture of tension and titillation, that impetus to release which could,

for a time, be cherished on a comfortable, gently swelling plateau—
I imagined her experiencing the same things, in the anatomically
female variant.

I was irrationally resentful of the fact that I wouldn't be able to
accompany her when she went. And it was a bit of a shock to note that
I cared more about my visions of Bernadette piddling voluminously
into the restaurant's sparkling toilet than I cared about the excellent
wine, the five-star food, or the urbane conversation. What, I wondered, would our friends think if they knew that the better part of my
consciousness was now turned toward meditations upon the joys my
wife feels when she holds her pee, along with rich conjectures regard-
ing what pleasures travel through her erogenous territories as she
releases it? They might be less inclined to pick up the tab, I supposed.

Despite my social qualms, my mind was drifting further and further from the restaurant chitchat. I found myself entertaining the
bizarre thought that it would be incredibly erotic for the two of us to
eschew the restrooms entirely and simply wet our pants in unison—or,
more accurately, in harmony, the alto and tenor ecstasies complement-
ing each other. It had never before crossed my mind to seek sexual
gratification through a fantasy of pissing in my clothes. But sitting
there at the elegant restaurant table, I had a strong vision of how magical it could be to watch Bernadette quietly piss herself, while feeling
a wet warmth in my own groin. I could vividly imagine how my own
physical bliss would give dimension to the voyeuristic thrill of studying her face as she sensuously wet herself. Ah, to hold her hand across
the table and watch her features relax as she gave in to her wetness.
Ah, to look under the table and see her little knees twitch and her cute

trousers darken at their feminine crotch, while I allowed a dedicated, complicit trickle of my own to approximate a shared experience.

Though this train of thought was making me hard, I was reasonable enough to see that this was a blueprint to file away for possible home use, and not one to bring to life in front of our friends in a restaurant. So I reluctantly set this fantasy aside before I came in my pants, peed in my pants, or both. It was then that my eyes met Bernadette's. She must have been observing my peculiarly preoccupied face, for her smile hinted at delight and curiosity.

She got up at last and headed in the appropriate direction for ladies who have been drinking much water and wine. I watched her handsomely trousered ass recede until she was out of sight. Then, while I feigned interest in a discussion of local jazz quartets, I wondered how thick and how forceful Bernadette's piss would be, how long it would continue, and how wide her smile would become as she enjoyed all the associated sensations. Would she touch herself, wishing I were with her? Would there be a woman in an adjoining stall who would hear a faint squeal of pleasure as Bernadette finished up? Would my wife's pelvis bounce as she made her last dribbles, or perhaps gyrate with tiny aftershocks?

My turn to leave the table came soon after Bernadette had reappeared, looking radiant. I had the men's room to myself. And, for the first time in my adult life, I elected to pee sitting down. In a convoluted twist on autoeroticism, I closed my eyes and pretended that I was Bernadette—pissing for me. It felt great; but I knew that we needed to go home and fuck before I drifted any further into an erotic haze.

By the time we arrived at the house, Bernadette was making it clear, with semi-masturbatory explicitness, that her bladder had long since forgotten the trip to the ladies' room. As had become typical, she made an uninhibited display of the enjoyable mixture of urgency and arousal that she experienced while holding on.

Hustling behind her jiggling ass as we traveled up the stairs, I felt that our evening out with our friends had been a mere prelude.

We entered the bedroom, and I turned on the light.

"Come on," she urged, pulling me forward toward the bathroom.

I stopped. It seemed so ridiculous, but I knew what I wanted. "Wait," I breathed. My heart raced to hear myself say it.

She giggled with a tipsy charm. "Derek, I'll wet my pants if I wait any longer."

"Yes," I said hopefully.

Her eyes widened.

"Unless you don't want to," I wavered.

I waited to see if she would rush for the toilet. But she froze in place. Her eyes lit up the room.

"Oh, Derek," was all she said when she dissolved into sensation. She shivered as she wholeheartedly relinquished control. An instant later, she was clutching frenetically at her pants, celebrating what was happening down there with bold, nurturing strokes.

Now it was my turn to freeze in place, as I watched her intimate waters seep through the crotch seam, rush down each leg, and puddle crazily onto the hardwood floor. It was, for the observer, a transcendent experience.

Bernadette was laughing, dancing and chanting. She was totally enthralled by her own act of sensual abandon. She was wetting her fucking pants for me, and she was having the time of her life doing it.

Eventually, with the vigorous flow still continuing, she peeled the trousers and clinging panties down so that I could see the inside story. I marveled at nature's sweet, gorgeous cascade. I admired it as it descended from the delirious pink pussy of a lady on the brink of knee-knocking orgasm, into the yearning geography of her woman-soaked clothing below.

It was Niagara Falls, with everything switched on.

ANDREA SEELY

TICKLING HER FANCY

EAST YOUR EYES ON THAT," Connor instructed me as he handed me a glossy brochure for an exotic vacation resort. "It's sure to tickle your fancy."

This was where he was taking me for our anniversary, and the surprise of being whisked away on a whim was thrilling. Even more so, however, was his choice of phrase, for I am an ardent fan of being tickled. This erotic activity sets me afire like nothing else. The word *tickling* alone is an aphrodisiac to me, conjuring up so many sexy images—from the delicious moments of anxious anticipation before the tickling begins, to the action itself, when Connor has me squirming fiercely on our bed, giggling uncontrollably and begging him for mercy. Of course he and I both know that I never really *want* mercy, but I do always beg.

Now, my interest was piqued. Was he taking me to some sort of tickle-lovers-only location? I could envision the scene in my mind:

beautiful naked women being pursued by men with feather dusters, bubbling laughter ringing out across an open atrium. Although the scenario was pure fiction, I couldn't wait to pack my bags!

"Did you say something about tickling?" I started softly, feeling a warmth between my legs.

He answered my query with a kiss, before brushing a strand of my long, auburn hair out of my jade eyes. "You'll love it, baby. I know you will."

He was right. Connor and I were both in awe when the taxi pulled up to our destination. Everything about the place whispered "paradise": the individual whitewashed buildings, the well-manicured lawns and sparkling fountains.

I glanced over at Connor as he took in the sights. My stunning husband looks great in a suit. But now that we were on vacation, he'd traded his corporate attire for faded jeans and a navy blue T-shirt. He appeared extremely relaxed as he pushed his shades up onto his dark hair and pointed toward our guesthouse.

"Just look at those," Connor said, and my gaze followed his outstretched arm. Each bungalow was surrounded by a garden filled with unusual flowers, and Connor was motioning to the lush pink blooms ringing our private cabana. The stalks were long and sturdy looking, almost like the stems of ferns, but the flowers themselves were neon pink explosions of the tiniest, thinnest petals I'd ever seen. When I got closer, I could see that the multitude of petals were almost like confetti, mere filigrees of flowers as dainty as snowflakes, their lush decorations ringing the building.

"I've never seen anything like them," Connor said as he ran his fingertips along one exquisite stalk, "but I know exactly how to use them."

My cheeks turned as bright pink as the long, feathery flowers, and I quickly unlocked the door to our unit and stepped inside. Connor brought in the suitcases and set them in the foyer, then went back outside again. I heard him rustling around in the foliage for several moments, and I felt my heart racing. When the door opened, he came inside, his arms filled with the long, delicate blooms.

"What are you doing, Connor?" I asked nervously. I could tell from his sexy expression that he wasn't simply presenting me, as his amour, with a bouquet of sweet nothings. This was clear from the look in his dreamy blue eyes and the cocky smile on his devilishly handsome face.

"What do *you* think I'm doing?" As he spoke, he began to trace the very tip of one of the flowers along my exposed collarbone. I playfully brushed the flower away, backing down the hallway with each step. Yet even as I moved away from him, I found that I was arching my body toward him ever so slightly. Each time he brought the petals to a new area of my skin, I felt kissed by the light sensation.

"You know you want it, baby," Connor admonished me, coming ever closer.

"Want what?" I asked, giggling already from the teasing tickling as I suddenly found myself in the bedroom, with nowhere else to go. Connor took immediate advantage of the situation. He dropped the bevy of feathery flowers onto the polished black nightstand and lifted me in his muscular arms. Quickly, he set me on the bed and untied the bow at the back of my red-and-white floral sundress. Within moments, he'd revealed the fact that I'd gone braless on our journey to this vacation spot.

"Such a naughty girl," Connor smiled as he reached for one of the long stalks. "Ready, baby?"

"Please," I said, begging already. But I wasn't begging him to stop—I was begging him to start.

"Anything you want," Connor assured me. "Just remember that you asked me to do this."

He used just the tip of the flowers to trace my apricot-hued nipples and I shivered all over at the wave of pleasure that instantly rushed through me. The lovely pink petals were as fine as angora fur, so sweet and soft I could hardly stand it. My thighs spread slightly, almost against my will, and I could feel already how wet I'd gotten, only from the initial brush of those feathers on my naked tits. What would happen when the ethereal blooms reached that sacred region between my legs?

"Oh, you love it, don't you?"

My eyes locked on my husband's as I felt the rush of arousal start to work more fiercely through me. Connor is my perfect mate: he loves to tickle me as much as I adore submitting to the powerful pleasure that his probing and tickling brings me. Whether he uses his hands, or a single feather, or one of my own marabou-trimmed nighties, he always teases me in just the right way, pushing me a bit beyond my previous limits each time we play. He likes the fact that he can reduce me to nothing more than a desire, an urge; that all of my thoughts become focused on the one task of taking in everything he dishes out and giving my pleasure over to him.

Now, he had a brand-new tool, and I could tell that he wanted to see what could be done with the fragrant all-natural sex toy. "What does it feel like, Sabrina?" he asked me.

"I don't know." My mind was hazy with the lust-drenched electric shivers already warming me up. For tickling enthusiasts such as me, the experience can be mind-altering. It's as if I enter a different frame of consciousness, in which my entire body is focused on the near-torturous yet extremely arousing action of being tickled and the release of fully submitting to that total-body sensation.

"Think," Connor insisted. "Tell me. I want to get inside your head—"

"A cloud," I said softly, closing my eyes to better see the images I was describing. "Something that's almost not even there. Fog or smoke or very fine lace."

"How about when I do this?" he asked, and now instead of using the tip of the flower, he used the entire stalk to caress my naked breasts. I sucked in my breath and held it, loving the way those tiny petals roamed over my nude body. The touch was almost maddening—so light, so delicate—and I reveled in every second of the sensuous experience. The way I felt from Connor massaging me with the flowers was akin to taking the very first bite of a decadent dessert. I knew that far more sweetness awaited me, but I savored every single moment.

Connor took his time, using two separate stems of flowers now to stroke my arms up and down. I gritted my teeth and held myself steady. A shiver ran down my spine as if Connor had lifted my heavy hair and kissed the very nape of my neck. The feeling of those tiny little flowers made me want to move, but at the same time, I had a deeper desire to sit exactly where I was and take every single second of the agonizingly sexy caresses. I could feel that my panties were very wet already, from this tiniest foray into tickling. I wondered if Connor could smell my scent over the light floral sweetness of the flowers.

Each time he stroked me with the petals, more of their aroma was freed into the room—and more of my own juicy sex cream followed immediately. A heady combination of the two scents surrounded me.

"You're incredibly wet, aren't you?" Connor whispered.

I nodded. "So wet, Connor. So fucking wet—"

"Your pussy's opening up just like these flowers. I can see it in my mind: those delicious inner lips of yours spreading open as you crave a stronger touch. Because that's what you want now, isn't it, Sabrina? A stronger touch."

He stroked the petals under my neck and I moaned and leaned my head back. I thought of the way Connor tickles me with our fancy feather dusters and with his own knowledgeable fingertips, and even with his thick dark hair, brushing between my inner thighs when he goes down on me. "Tell me," he insisted.

"Tell you what?" My brain was concentrating only on my cunt. I couldn't think straight.

"Tell me all about that gorgeous pussy of yours—"

"I'm dripping," I told him. "Just like you said. Each time you touch me with those flowers, my pussy lips spread even wider apart." I rocked my hips back and forth as I spoke, and I could feel the slippery wetness seeping through my panties.

"Take off your dress and thong," Connor demanded.

I followed his order in no time, pushing the fabric over my hips and kicking the dress to the floor, then losing my silver thong in equal record speed. I was desperate to feel those flowers all over my naked body. I wanted Connor to tickle me harder, so that the petals would crush against me, releasing their inner perfume as I released mine.

"Lie down, Sabrina, and clasp your hands over your head," Connor continued, "and keep them there."

"Or what?" I asked, knowing that I was being daring by pushing him.

"Or I'll stop," he assured me. "You don't want me to stop, do you, baby? Not even if the tickling is driving you crazy. Not even if you think you need me to stop—just for a moment, just for a second to let you catch your breath. You don't really want me to, do you? You never really want me to, do you?"

"No," I admitted. This was the truth. Even when my entire body is shaking with uncontrollable spasms of laughter and I feel physically wrenched by the experience, I don't want him to stop. I want him to take me to the furthest reaches of bliss—and I can get there only by submitting to his desires...and to my own.

"Then do as I say."

Obediently, I lay back on the firm, king-sized mattress and locked my hands together over my head. I was offering him my underarms and my ribs, two extremely sensitive regions, but I trusted Connor not to abuse his power over me.

"Where do you want to feel the petals?" he asked softly.

I thought for a moment. Then, honestly, I said, "Everywhere."

"But where do you want them first?" he prompted. "Tell me what you want, and I'll make your wish come true."

I lifted my upper body off the bed, offering him my entire torso. "You know," I told him. "Under my arms. And down my ribs. And then—" my voice shook as I got ready to say it. "Oh, God, Connor, and then run them over my pussy lips. I want to feel them against my skin there, lightly caressing me there—"

"Wait, baby," Connor admonished me. "We'll get there. Don't worry. You know I'll take care of that pretty pussy of yours. Just let me go at my own speed."

I nodded, understanding that he was going to take his time and loving him for it.

Gently, Connor began to stroke the feathery blooms along my ribs, using the flowers like wands, running the edges all the way to my underarms and then back down to the indent of my waist. I started laughing now, squirming on the mattress from the way those feathery petals tickled. This was such a new feeling for me. Yes, I've been tickled many times in the past. Connor knows how much I like this extreme form of submission. Being tickled brings me to the very pinnacle of pleasure. My pussy seems to absorb the sensations no matter where they occur. Even when he's tickling my toes, or the curve of my neck, I feel the rumbling effects pulsing deep inside my cunt. Being tickled by Connor makes my orgasms resonate in every part of my body. Nothing compares to that experience.

But this time was different because the tool was so unique. The petals almost felt like tiny fingertips trailing all over my ribs and then down the flat of my belly to my pussy—my waiting, hungry pussy. I groaned so loud when Connor ran the flowers over my bikini region that I startled myself. He kept using the two stalks back and forth, first one, then the other, and then he used one over my breasts, caressing my pebble-like nipples while the other strand of flower petals tapped and rapped along my clit. He brought that stalk between my legs, so the sweet furlike petals tickled my inner thighs, and I groaned ferociously and arched my hips for him, knowing how urgent I looked, how reckless and open my whole body had become.

"Wait for it, Sabrina," Connor said, never stopping the rotations of those petals. When he used them on my inner thighs, I started giggling louder. I was helpless in seconds, rocking back and forth on the bed, but I didn't let go of my locked hands.

"Hold still," Connor admonished me, yet I couldn't. The feathery flowers tickled so bad and so good at the same time. But each stroke raised me up one more notch closer to climax, and I gave in to him. I could feel it happen. That's the best part about being tickled, for me. The moment of utter release and the freedom of giving in. I could feel how my ribs hurt from laughing, how my whole body ached in a delicious way. And now I could feel the surrender.

Tickle me, I thought. *Go on, Connor, tickle me until I come!*

As if he could read my dirty desires, he did just that. First one strand of petals kissed over my clit, then the other, back and forth, and then, at the moment he could sense that I needed an even stronger touch, he let go of the flowers entirely and brought his fingers into play. He used one hand to continue to lightly tickle my soft inner thighs, and with the other hand he parted my pussy lips wide. The swollen lips let him know how aroused I was. His tongue against my clit found out that secret even more. My pussy swam with sexy juices, and Connor's tongue carefully licked and lapped at me. In the same rhythm as he'd used to tickle me with the flowers, he now tickled me with the very tip of his tongue.

"Oh, yes," I sighed, nearly sobbing, partly laughing. "Oh, yes, Connor. Do that. That!"

Connor rubbed his head back and forth, and his soft hair delighted me as always, the edges flicking over my most tender skin, tickling my nether regions as his tongue continued to make its wild, tantalizing trip. I sealed myself to him, raising my hips and then wrapping my legs around his neck. I bucked and arched, and he brought both hands up higher now, using his short nails to graze against my ribs so that I was in tickling hell—or tickling heaven—laughing with abandon as I came on his face, rocking him to the rhythm of my choosing now and coming, coming, coming.

But even when I crested and slipped back down into the paradise-scented pool of pleasure, Connor didn't show any signs of letting up. His relentless fingers actually pressed harder as he continued to tickle me. Laughing with abandon, I squirmed in his embrace and tried to pull away, but Connor was in charge.

The long journey to our vacation spot had made me ready for release. I guess Connor must have felt the same way, because the look in his eyes let me know that he wasn't going to stop until both of us had reached our limits. He lifted his mouth off me just long enough to swivel into a sixty-nine position. And then he said, "I want to feel them, too—"

He didn't have to give me any more instruction than that. I fumbled behind me for one of the abandoned stalks of flowers. Then using the lightest possible touch I began to rub the millions of tiny silky blooms against Connor's balls. He sighed so deeply that the whole bed shook.

"Oh, God," he whispered. "Oh, Sabrina—"

I kept up the caressing with the petals, envisioning exactly what he was feeling. I knew perfectly well how surprising the softness of the petals felt against that most tender skin. Connor loved every second of the petal-massage.

"Don't stop!" he said, and I wouldn't have even if he'd remained silent. I could tell by the way his entire body had stiffened that he was more turned on than I'd ever seen him before. "It's like thousands of tiny fingers—" he exclaimed, his mouth only a sliver of space away from my pussy. "Or tongues. Or something—"

"Something," I murmured, agreeing with the statement as I opened my mouth and drew his cock inside. My warm mouth connected with the warmth of his skin, and I traced my tongue along the length of his shaft before swallowing down on him. I continued to use the flowers to cradle and tap at his balls as my mouth sucked hard on his rod. Connor didn't seem to know what to do. He was reaching ecstasy, and he gripped his fingers into my skin, fucking my mouth as I played those dreamy games with the stalks of pretty blooms.

I thought of how Connor had used the flowers on me, lightly and then more firmly, and I altered the pressure with which I stroked his balls. I knew that some of the tickling flower petals were finding the valley between his asscheeks and caressing him there, and this image—combined with the heady contact of his tongue on my clit— made me come for a second time. My orgasm flared through me like a whirlwind, ricocheting inside of me, and I swallowed even harder on Connor and let the flowers stroke him in a stronger fashion. This combination of tactile pleasures brought him to his peak, and when he came, he groaned out loud, calling out my name as the sheer thrill of it all flooded through him. "Oh, yes, Sabrina!" he moaned. "Oh, yes." His whole body shook, and then he fell back on the bed and sighed deeply.

I looked at him, smiling and blushing at the same time, and then I looked around at the scattered flower petals. Each time we'd played with the long stalks, the flowers had shed, the tiny petals covering the comforter in a snowstorm of pink petal shreds. It was as if we'd made love on a bed of the tiny, fragrant blooms. The scene was both beautiful and debauched, which is how a lot of scenarios are for me and my man.

After a moment, I lay back next to him, crushing petals underneath me and smelling their lush fragrance perfuming the air. My body felt tender all over from being so lightly but perfectly tickled and my pussy still tightened and opened with powerful echoes of the pleasure that Connor—and those magical flowers—had brought me. But as my head started to clear, I realized something that I should have understood from the beginning.

"*You* chose the place, Connor," I said, suddenly guessing that he'd had ulterior motives the whole time. "You must have seen those flowers in one of the promotional photos, right? Is that what made you pick this resort for our vacation?"

He just gave me his most charming smile and reached to bring me into a tight embrace.

THOMAS S. ROCHE

SWITCHBLADE

ROM L7 TO DIAMANDA to Christian Death, the music cast auditory shadows across the crowd, raking the listeners' souls with long fingernails. Kylie stalked the darkness to the beat, seeking her prey.

She wore a tight leather vest with nothing underneath, the sides of her slight breasts visible through the armholes, a small amount of cleavage evident in the deep V of its front. If the leather had been of slightly lower quality, you wouldn't have been able to see the nipples through the buttery black midnight—growing more evident and visible, demanding, defiant, whenever Kylie felt them hardening. The two bottom buttons of the leather vest—undone—came six inches short of Kylie's low-slung leather jeans, showing the tattooed white belly and the bright ring through the navel, challenging anyone to dare to think of this woman, just for one second, as an ornament. The leather pants, starting two inches below the navel and unhindered by anything underneath, were not quite tight enough to show the outline of Kylie's cunt, the swell of her lips and their rings. The pants zipped down the back between the globes of Kylie's ass, eternally unzipped just a quarter-inch, just enough to invite the casual passerby to start on unzipping them the rest of the way—if she dared. That potential energy put Kylie in absolute erotic control of her world, knowing that the invitation went unanswered for want of nerve, not desire.

Kylie's hair was shaved on the sides of her head, showing the supple tattoo of blue-black chain curving around silver-flashing ears.

She was an imposing woman. Although only five foot three, and barely one hundred pounds, her power emanated from some sort of inner reservoir. That, and the barest hint of the knife that showed at the top of her boot. It was a switchblade, and it radiated the covert power given off by all contraband weapons—only in a club like this could Kylie wear it with impunity, even half-secreted as it was.

Lisette stood there against the mirror, caressed by the shadows from the dance floor, afraid and mesmerized. Her baby-doll dress was short, as Kylie had insisted, and tight, as she had strongly suggested. Lisette's nipples showed through the thin cotton. Laced halfway to her knees were the combat boots she had mentioned one night, months ago, that had brought such an impressive and approving string of expletives from Kylie's fast-moving fingers.

Remembering the words, Lisette shivered.

Slowly, Kylie made her way across the edge of the dance floor, casually studying the scene. She didn't need to elbow people aside, but as the crowd grew thicker, passage became more difficult. She paused in one corner, her back to Lisette.

Lisette looked, breathing hard, blinking to make sure it was real. Her wrists were crossed behind her; the hot smell of sex was in her nostrils. She could feel the tension in her hips, feel the tingling in her fingertips. Her lips and tongue were dry. She shot a glance toward the door, wondering how fast she could get back to her hotel and masturbate, or if she could manage to do it on the street without anyone noticing. Then she licked her lips and reached for the zipper on the back of the woman's jeans. Her hands shaking, Lisette pulled the zipper awkwardly down the center of Kylie's ass, to the very top of her crack, the tight leather peeling insistently away, the white flesh smooth and sweat-slick underneath. Kylie was like a mannequin, waiting.

The zipper reached the halfway point, and Lisette stopped.

A laugh worked its way underneath the throbbing beat of Tribe 8, as Kylie threw her head back. She turned her head only just enough for Lisette to hear her. "Your name had better be Lisette," said Kylie.

The press of women was tight all around them. Lisette looked at Kylie, turned now to face her. Kylie's cold steel eyes mercilessly opened up that baby-doll dress.

"Kylie," said Lisette.

The blood-red lips, the bottom one pierced with a 16-gauge labrette, parted deliciously, savoring the taste of a morsel not yet devoured. Kylie licked them with a red tongue, also pierced.

"Pleased to meet you," said Kylie, sliding forward to kiss Lisette and let her hands creep around the swell of the girl's breasts, right there on the edge of the dance floor. Lisette melted into Kylie's hands.

Kylie's place was not far away, and she wasn't really in the mood for dancing. They didn't talk much—they had talked enough already, and neither one could afford to break the spell Kylie had cast. Lisette walked three paces behind Kylie, hypnotized by the sway of her white flesh exposed beneath the half-opened zipper and at the terminus of the black leather vest.

They had to pass through an alley to get to the place. Suddenly Lisette gasped as Kylie turned on her, slamming her against the smooth concrete wall with the full force of that leather-clad body. Kylie pressed against Lisette, grinding against the ephemeral cotton of the baby-doll dress. She kissed Lisette hard, thrusting her tongue into the sub's mouth and then suckling hungrily on her lower lip. Lisette whimpered while Kylie reached down the front of her dress, feeling her breast, rubbing and pinching the hardness of her nipple. With the other hand, she reached under the dress, sliding around Lisette's ass and squeezing, then working her fingers around and pressing them between Lisette's thighs.

Lisette wasn't wearing even the barest whisper of underwear, and Kylie's two fingers slid easily into the pretty girl's cunt while her thumb worked her clit. Lisette's mouth opened wide in a gasp of stunned pleasure as Kylie pressed her fingers home. Kylie kissed Lisette again, rougher this time, biting her lower lip and smearing lipstick haphazardly. She slid her fingers out of Lisette's cunt and lifted them to Lisette's lips, stroking gently. Lisette licked Kylie's fingers, tasting herself.

Kylie moved both hands down the dress now, pulling two of her buttons open. Lisette pressed herself against the wall, not daring to move her own hands, as Kylie felt her ample breasts, squeezing gently and then pinching the nipples roughly. Tweaking them. Now the dress was open halfway down the front, and the cool night air was caressing Lisette's body.

Kylie took her hands out of the dress and stood there looking at the sub in the faint moonlight, at the exposed mounds of her tits and the white belly. She pressed forward once more, up close, one hand on Lisette's tit, the other reaching down smoothly as she lifted her foot.

The switchblade slid smoothly out of the well-oiled boot sheath, open without a sound and up against Lisette's face, bright blade flickering in the moonlight.

"Upstairs," she said, as she turned and walked away down the alley. The switchblade had vanished like a whisper.

Lisette buttoned her dress up quickly before she hurried to follow Kylie, but she missed a few buttons in her haste.

It was an attic studio, nested atop two flights of stairs over the office of a queer nonprofit. A single room, empty except for the necessities: bed, chair, chains, restraints. The finish on the hardwood floor was worn away to white in the spot under the eyehole; the black leather restraints hung on a chain above the worn patch.

"Turn around and walk out," said Kylie, "if that's what you want. No hard feelings."

Lisette had long ago given up that option, and she shook her head quickly, the blood throbbing in her head.

Kylie shrugged and smiled. "Then you know the drill."

Lisette did. She was revealed only in the flickering lights of the city and the headlamps from cars heading into the hills. Breathless, she reached up and undid the buttons of the baby-doll dress.

She opened it up slowly, sensuously, shrugged the dress off and stood there naked except for boots, nervously holding the dress in front of her. Kylie nodded approvingly.

Lisette put the dress on the floor near the door. She took off her boots and socks, and left them there next to the dress. Then she walked over to the bare spot on the floor.

Kylie watched as Lisette put her wrists in the leather restraints, buckling them just tightly enough and then snapping the padlocks shut. She had a lot of trouble with the second restraint, and especially with the second padlock. Kylie did not move to help her.

Lisette had no piercings, no tattoos. Kylie liked knowing that this was an untouched body begging to be marked and that she would exercise all the restraint necessary to make not a single discoloration on that expanse of virgin skin. Damn, this dyke was beautiful.

Her lips parted, lush and inviting; her body grew charged with desire. Lisette knew she had sealed her fate, and almost without knowing she was doing it, she spoke, answering the unanswered question.

"I trust you," she said, her voice husky.

Kylie smiled as Lisette stood there naked and chained, whimpering faintly in the midnight. She began to walk toward her. A vicious laugh, delighting in mayhem and the sound of broken glass. The switchblade appeared in Kylie's hand.

"Trust whoever you want," Kylie said—the point of the switchblade straying dangerously close to Lisette's jugular—"You belong to me now."

Kylie pressed her body against Lisette's, stroking the vulnerable white throat. She let her tongue laze out and lightly touch Lisette's cheek. Lisette could feel the swell of Kylie's breasts through the leather vest, feel the smoothness of Kylie's left hand against her bare belly. Feel the insistence with which Kylie reached down and slipped a hand between Lisette's legs.

Gently, two of Kylie's fingers explored the slick flesh of Lisette's cunt. She slipped both fingers in, making Lisette slump in the restraints.

"Don't start that shit," growled Kylie, grasping Lisette's hair. "Potential nerve damage. On your feet, woman."

Guided by the force of Kylie's fingers inside her, Lisette steadied herself, taking the pressure off her restrained wrists, locking her knees.

"Not that, either," whispered Kylie, grinning as she slid her fingers gently in and out of Lisette's body. "Haven't you heard the stories about altar boys? Lock your knees and next thing you know, you'll be out cold. Or maybe you *want* to be an altar boy." Kylie's fingers pumped a torturous rhythm in and out of Lisette, invading and nurturing. Her other hand was curved around Lisette's neck, holding the blade against her throat.

"Wanna be an altar boy?" Kylie was not quite smiling.

Lisette managed to shake her head, faintly, and unlock her knees. Kylie's thumb came down in a semicircle and pressed, lightly, against the hard bud of Lisette's clit.

Kylie's lips were now so close to Lisette's ear that they moved against the flesh as she spoke. Pressed together as they were, the razor edge of the quicksilver blade touched both their throats, and only Kylie's iron control prevented the rending of flesh.

"As I was saying…" said Kylie, drawing the edge of the blade across Lisette's throat, awakening her skin, "…this is act one of a morality play."

Slowly, Kylie drew the edge of the knife along Lisette's parted lips, gently prodding the very tip of her tongue. Her other hand absently caressed the full breasts and worked the swollen nipples, the pressure growing harder as Lisette's whimpering moans gained volume and desperation. Her breasts were extremely sensitive, Kylie knew, though not from experience; long, slow, rhythmic nipple play with the slightest pressure on her clit could make Lisette come even if she was standing up. Kylie knew this, and she was using it for everything it was worth. Lisette's eyes were wide open, staring into Kylie's as the knife entered her, the tip just grazing the roof of her mouth.

"Danger is such a luxury for a woman," mused Kylie, as if reciting the only lines to the morality play she'd composed in her head, her pierced tongue flickering in an unusually erotic and serpentine fashion, "when she is absolutely and totally safe."

Lisette could taste the sharp tang of the metal, could feel Kylie's power as she stroked her tongue with the flat of the blade. Gradually, Lisette felt it coming on, and she knew that only Kylie could stop it. Her eyes flickered and Kylie seemed to know, seemed to sense what was happening. The pinching of her nipples grew stronger, faster, the rhythmic squeeze more insistent. Smoothly, Kylie slipped the blade out of Lisette's mouth, drawing it slick across her cheek and then down her belly, spreading her fingers as she pressed it flat against the front of Lisette's pubic bone.

"Come, you bitch," growled Kylie as her fingers pressed hard on Lisette's clit, and that's exactly when Lisette did.

She had come standing up many times before, but this time was different. It was so hard to stand up when all she wanted to do was to give in to this woman, surrender to her, lie under her feet and be caressed by the power of her silver blade. Lisette moaned faintly as she came, hard and fast, and finally her knees gave out. Kylie was ready even before Lisette was; the blade disappeared as Kylie threw it to pierce the wood of the far wall, where it stood out, perpendicular and quivering. Kylie's other hand left Lisette's breast, reaching up and hitting the quick-release so that Lisette fell into her embrace. Within a few seconds Lisette was laid out on the floor, Kylie kneeling over, propping a small pillow under her head, and setting the other woman's bound wrists on her stomach just beneath her breasts.

The faint spasms of Lisette's orgasm were still surging through her. She felt safe in a way she had not felt for a long time. Kylie was over her, holding a squeeze bottle of grape juice, offering broken-off morsels of Saltine cracker. Lisette looked up into darkness and saw only the serpentine twistings of Kylie's body as she unfastened the padlocks.

It was what Kylie expected, and what Lisette had demanded so many weeks ago across the electronic frontier that had separated them. That she should succumb so completely after the torture, that the rest of the night would be spent in luxurious nothingness. But Lisette, surprising even herself, did not sleep. When she thought about it later, her memories were dimmed, clouded and obscured as they were by a desire so acute it obliterated her mind. She remembered Kylie undressing at the side of the bed, the buttery black leather peeling away from the tight breasts and tattooed legs, the gentle scissor of Kylie's thighs as she climbed onto the futon, her tongue tracing the faintest path up Lisette's throat to her mouth, then plumbing its depths insistently. Kylie was surprised when Lisette asked with a faint, desirous whisper for Kylie to make love to her, to fuck her until she couldn't be fucked anymore. Smiling faintly but still very serious, Kylie said, "Act two."

Kylie did just as Lisette had asked, spreading her legs over Lisette and settling the pierced cunt down on Lisette's seeking mouth and tongue. Then, eagerly, Kylie lowered her face and worked her own tongue into Lisette, building on the tiny spasms which still occasionally went through the succulent flesh. Kylie was the one to come first, and she found herself doing it a second time before Lisette climaxed again herself.

Wrapped in each other, they began to fall asleep as the apartment flooded with diffuse light. One hand on Lisette's breast, Kylie counted down the number of things she knew about this woman. Residence, New York City. Account name lisette@dom.com. Stage name Selena Montage. Real name? Who the fuck knew? No piercings, no tattoos, no distinguishing marks; no whips, no spanking, no bruises, no hickeys. Back in New York, she topped men and women for a living, a well-known and respected young dom with a tendency toward extreme cruelty. An excellent top, but also a private switch with a fondness for the edge. They had thirteen transcontinental friends in common, Kylie knew, a very lucky number. Lisette had checked with them all concerning Kylie's reliability and reputation—Lisette, it seemed, was a very careful woman.

They had said so few words to each other—the weeks of text-only communication had perhaps filled much of that need. Kylie wondered if they would talk over breakfast. Kylie wondered if Lisette was fond of omelettes.

Light started to break through the apartment, but it was not yet dawn.

THE DEATH OF THE
MARABOU SLIPPERS

FEATHERS. Pink-tipped white feathers.

The feathers transformed the shoes from any other innocent pair of bedroom slippers into true decadence. But maybe they weren't quite so innocent to start with. Maybe they knew what they were doing all along. You've seen the type—smug in their open-toedness. Willful in their daring high-heeled glory. Deliciously trimmed with a bit of tender white-pink marabou fluff on the front, just to get your attention.

I'd never owned shoes like these before. Sure, I'd seen versions of them in the Frederick's of Hollywood catalog, insolently positioned with toe toward the camera, daring the casual peruser to purchase them. And I'd even drooled over such fantasy footwear when it was worn by my favorite forties screen stars: Myrna Loy. Claudette Colbert. Garbo. But those women had the clothes to go with the shoes—angel-sleeved nightgowns with three-foot trains, tight satin slips with plunging necklines. Such sexy slippers weren't meant for someone like me—a girl who owns plain white bra and panty sets, who wears Gap sweats to bed, whose one experience with a pair of black fishnets was a comedic disaster.

What purpose could a pair of wayward shoes like these possibly have?

Still, when I caught sight of the immoral mules at a panty sale in San Francisco, I bought them. Even though they were a size 8 and I'm a size 6. Even though I found the very sight of them fairly wicked. Even though my own bedroom slippers at home were made of plaid flannel and had been chewed on repeatedly by my golden retriever puppy.

I simply thought Lucas would like them.

He did.

"I'm gonna fuck those shoes," he said when I pulled them from the silver bag. "Sweetheart, those shoes are history."

I'd never seen him react like that to anything. My tall, handsome, green-eyed husband has a healthy libido. I definitely get my share of bedroom romping time. But as far as kinkiness goes, he has always appeared positively fetish-free. No requests for handcuffs. No need for teddies or "special" outfits to get him in the mood. No urgent trips to Safeway at midnight for whipped cream, chocolate sauce, and maraschino cherries.

"Put them on," Lucas hissed. "Now."

I kicked off my patent leather penny loafers, pulled off my black stockings, and slid into the marabou mules. The white-pink bit of fluff on the toes made the shoes look like some sort of pastry, a fantasy confection created just for feet. My red toenails peeked through the opening.

Dirty, I thought. *Indecent.*

Lucas got on the floor and kissed my exposed toes, stroked the soft feathery tips of the shoes, then stood and quickly shed his clothes.

"They're bad," he said excitedly, positioning himself between my parted legs, his cock over my feet, as if preparing to do push-ups. He's ex-military and has excellent formation for this activity—his body becomes stiff and boardlike. The sleek muscles in his back shift becomingly under his tan skin. In this position, his straining cock went directly between the two mules.

"Oh, man," he whispered. "So bad they're good."

He went up and down over my shoes, digging his cock between them, dragging it over the marabou trim, sighing with delight when the feathers got between his legs. I could only imagine how those pale white feathers tickled his most sensitive organ.

"They're so soft," he murmured.

I'd been staring down at him, at his fine ass—clenching with each depraved push-up—at his strong back, the muscles rippling. Now, I looked straight ahead, into the full-length mirror across the room, taking in the total effect of our afternoon of debauchery.

I was fully dressed: long black skirt, black mock turtleneck, my dark hair in a refined ponytail, small spectacles in place. If you ended the reflection at my shins, you might have placed me for exactly what I am, an editor at an educational publishing company. Below my shins, however, was Lucas, doing ungodly push-ups over my brand-new shoes. My slim ankles were bare, feet sliding slightly in the too-big marabou-trimmed mules. If you disregarded the shoes, and imagined Lucas moving in stop-motion animation, he might have been culled from a series of Eadweard Muybridge pictures. But with the shoes in place, and with Lucas's body moving rigidly up and down, this picture looked more like something from a fantastic pornographic movie.

I stared at our images and felt myself growing more and more aroused. My plain white panties were suddenly too containing. I needed my skirt and sweater to come off. Arousal rushed through me in a shuddering wave. But I kept my peace—this wasn't my fantasy, wasn't my moment. It was Lucas's. All his.

He began speaking louder, first lauding the shoes, "Sweet, so sweet." Then criticizing the slippers as he slammed between them: "Oh, you're bad...bad."

I stayed as still as possible, watching in awe as Lucas, approaching his limit, arched up and sat back on his heels, his hand working his cock in double-time. Small bits of pure white feathers were stuck to the sticky tip of his swollen penis. More feather fluffs floated in the air around us.

"Give me one of the shoes," he demanded, and I kicked off the right slipper. One hand still wrapped around his cock, he used the other to lift the discarded shoe and began rubbing the tip of it between his legs, moaning and sighing, his words no longer intelligible, no longer necessary. Then suddenly, as if inspiration had hit him, he reached behind his body with the shoe, poking the heel of it between the cheeks of his ass, impaling himself with the slipper while he dragged the tip of his cock against the shoe I still wore.

I watched closely as his breathing caught, as he leaned back further still and then came, ejaculating on the slipper before him, coating those naughty feathers with semen, matting the feathers into a sticky mess. Showing them once and for all who was boss.

When he had relaxed enough to speak, he looked up at me, a sheepish expression on his face. "Told you those shoes were history," he said, red-cheeked. Embarrassed. "Told you, baby, didn't I?"

I just nodded, thinking: The death of an innocent pair of marabou slippers. What'd the shoes ever do to Lucas? Nothing but exist.

JOLENE HUI

THE TALE OF MAGENTA AND SILVER

FUCK. I REALLY NEEDED TO COME. My jaw was tense and my pussy felt tight and anxious. Wednesday, I had gone out with Robert and we'd had a decent dinner at a little café by my house. He was an accountant and loved his work. However, he often played hard. He told me his nose was hurting from the cocaine he had enjoyed last weekend. I laughed when he described waking up on a strange purple couch at an unknown location. He had taken his tie off by the end of our meal. I noticed it when we were finishing off our wine.

We'd been dating for three months and so far I hadn't had an orgasm with him. And I can't say it was his fault. He fucked like a rock star. His days as a fraternity house stud were still apparent. Everything about him was attractive to me. His cock was big, thick, and smooth, and he kept himself trimmed perfectly.

But still, no magic O for me.

After our wine we had walked back to my place and immediately started making out on the couch. I could feel his hardness pushing against my thigh so I decided to let it free. There was nothing I liked better than a big hard cock. I positioned my mouth over it and sucked. He moaned slightly and I gripped the base with my left hand and moved it deep inside my mouth. We quickly stripped our clothes off and I ran into my bedroom, jumping over piles of shoes and miraculously making it to my nightstand in the dark. I knew exactly where the condoms were: snuggling right next to my friends Magenta and Silver.

Silver was the little clit massager my sister got me for my birthday and Magenta was a nice, small, penis-shaped vibe I'd bought as a Valentine's Day present for myself last year. I had the best orgasms with Magenta. When I didn't feel like doing much work, I'd use Silver, as he was equipped with a nice remote control. I could just put him right in my underwear against my clit and lie back and relax.

"Don't worry, guys, I'll see you later," I promised as I closed the drawer.

I ran out to the living room to find Robert lighting a candle on the coffee table. The light glowed nicely. I was convinced that tonight would be the night I'd have an earth-shattering orgasm from his cock.

"I really love the mood lighting." I walked over to him and held out the condom.

"I just wanted to see your hot body," he said grabbing it. "Get on your hands and knees."

I obeyed. I could hear him rolling on the condom. His tongue hit my clit immediately when he got to the floor. How did he find it so quickly? How was he such an expert?

I arched my back as he worked his tongue in and out until I was good and wet. Then he shifted positions, and when he slammed his cock into me I was ready. He put his hands around my waist and moved me to him. He flipped me every way he could and we were covered in sweat. He played with my clit, withdrew his cock and used his mouth, used his fingers in ungodly ways that made me scream, but I couldn't come. Finally, after what seemed like forever, he came and collapsed on top of me.

"I'm sorry, baby," he said, "I just couldn't take it any longer."

"It's not your fault," I said. "I know."

He left right after that and I took a shower to wash the sweat off of my body. My pussy felt worn out but I could still feel the tension. As soon as I slipped into bed, I opened my drawer, grabbed Magenta and turned out the light.

"Come here, sweet baby," I whispered. "Make me feel good."

It took only a minute. I worked it around my clit as it buzzed lightly. As soon as I slipped it in, I felt the waves start. "Oh yes, I love you," I said and fell asleep with Magenta in my hand.

I awoke refreshed. I was supposed to see Robert the following evening, but I wasn't sure if I could handle it. Of course, I could introduce him to my friends Magenta and Silver, but I didn't know if I wanted to share such a secret yet. I was a little protective of them. I popped Silver in my purse in case I needed a pick-me-up on my lunch hour.

I was at my desk with Silver between my legs when Robert called. Maybe a little training was all I needed. If I could train myself, then I'd be sure to come with him when we next got together.

"Hey you," I answered, my voice slightly wavering.

"What's up?"

"Oh...um...nothing." I was coming.

"Do you still want to meet up tomorrow?"

I was silent, swallowing and enjoying the feelings pouring from my pussy.

"Are you still there?"

I clicked the switch to OFF and decided to answer. Did I want to introduce him to Silver and Magenta? "Sure. I have a couple of friends I want to introduce you to."

"Really? Should I make a reservation for four?"

"No, just come on over."

"You making something?"

"Not really."

By the time Friday had rolled around, I had washed Magenta and Silver and prepared them to meet Robert.

"You two ready?"

I put on a short red dress and went out to the living room to set the table. I was so determined to have an orgasm with Robert that I'd have to let him into my private world with Magenta and Silver.

I ordered dinner from this fantastic catering company. I worked too much to cook. When Robert came over, he was surprised that I was hanging out alone. He had, obviously, expected another couple.

"Where are the others?" He asked.

"They're in the bedroom," I answered.

Clearly aroused, he started kissing me immediately and backed me into the bedroom. Magenta and Silver were perched on the bed. I pulled away from Robert. "I wanted to show you my friends."

I pulled away and he laughed, pulling my panties off and unzipping his pants.

"Wait, I'm serious." I leapt onto the bed.

His erect dick pointed at me. He said, "Looks like we're all alone."

I reached over and grabbed my vibes. "These make me come. Do you want to use them?"

A look of slight confusion passed over his face and then melted into a smile. He said, "Sure, baby, bring them over here."

Robert grabbed Magenta and turned her on. I got wet just hearing the buzzing start. I leaned onto my elbows and spread my thighs. He gently placed it against my clit and started to move it around a bit. "Am I doing this right, baby?" he whispered.

"Oh yeah, keep on doing what you're doing."

I closed my eyes and let him massage my clit and then work it inside me and out. When I was about to come I opened my eyes and told him to put it inside me. I came hard, the liquid squirting onto his fingers and all over Magenta. My knees shook with satisfaction. My pussy was so wet that when his cock slid in, it felt fantastic. He pumped for a while and then pulled out and came on me. After we washed up we ate the catered food in bed.

The next day, I was playing with Silver in my car at lunch when he called.

"I'm coming over tonight," he said.

I had just planned on having a nice night at home alone—maybe with a movie and a pizza. But I was fond enough of him, so I agreed.

When he showed up I had already started without him. Silver was against my clit and my arms were above my head. I was moaning when he walked into the room. I could see the excitement in his eyes. I was completely naked, my golden skin shiny from the sweat. These vibrators seemed to be taking a lot of my time lately. Even on breaks from work I was completely involved in using them. Whenever I needed to release stress, I seemed to go to them for help. They were my best friends, my lovers, and everything I really needed. What would I do without them?

Robert took his clothes off and straddled me. I moved Silver around my clit and he grabbed himself. "I wanna be inside you," he said, but I was enjoying myself too much.

"Gotta wait 'til next time," I said.

He tugged even harder. "But I want to feel myself inside you."

"Oh, baby, just wait a little longer," I said, moving Silver around my wet pussy.

"Why don't you turn on your stomach and let me in your ass?"

I gave him a dirty look. "Just let me come like this!"

He didn't say a thing, but kept tugging away at himself. I closed my eyes and let the feelings take me away. A sound of pleasure escaped my lips. When I opened my eyes, Robert shot his cum in my hair.

"You fucker," I said, grabbing a tissue.

He ended up leaving and I sat in my recliner and watched a movie.

A couple of weeks later I got home anxious to spend some time with Magenta. I felt like I'd been neglecting her for a while. I hadn't talked to Robert since he'd marched out. I didn't need someone im my life who was jealous of my vibrators. How silly was that? They were just toys. Weren't they? When I opened my nightstand drawer, it was empty. I went into a panic.

Maybe they weren't just toys. I knew I hadn't taken them anywhere out of the ordinary. I checked my purse to find Silver wrapped in a delicate towel but Magenta was nowhere. I never took her anywhere anyway so it would be weird that she was missing. I looked through every drawer in every room: bedroom, bathroom, kitchen, living room. Nothing. I couldn't find anything. My heart was racing.

Where was she?

I sat in my recliner to think about it. When had I used her last? It had to have been a couple of days ago. I had used her after my shower when I'd come home from a late meeting at work. Last night I was out late with my best friend. She and I went out the last Tuesday of every month just to catch up. I had come home and crashed. I had been drunk and exhausted. But I hadn't checked to make sure she was there. What could have happened to her?

Then I realized my mistake.

I had given Robert a spare key to my place.

Could he have come in and taken Magenta? I was furious just thinking about it. We had parted on bad terms. I knew he had been jealous of my relationship with Magenta. He knew about the monthly appointment I had with my friend. Would he have done that? Just to get back at me?

Anger overcame me. I jumped in my car and drove straight to his house to confront him.

I tried to take deep breaths on his doorstep, but I pounded on the door, my face bright red.

"Hey, what are you doing here?" He looked extremely confused.

I knew I looked angry. "Are you going to tell me what happened?"

"What?" He looked behind him, then stepped out onto the patio and closed the door.

"You know what I'm talking about, Robert!"

He looked mildly scared.

"I have no idea what you're talking about. Could you keep your voice down?" He put his hands on my shoulders and backed me toward the stairs.

"Get your hands off of me, you thief!"

"I didn't steal anything." He tried to get me to go down the stairs.

"Are you using her with your new girlfriend, you sick fuck?"

"You need to leave, now." He started to push me toward my car.

I shook free and slapped him across the face. "You know what I'm talking about, you filthy bastard, and I think you're disgusting."

"You are out of your mind," he said. "Get in your car and get out of here or I'm calling the cops."

I was stunned that I'd actually slapped him. I didn't say anything and got into my car. My nose was running. I'd left my purse on the passenger seat. I had to blow my nose before I started the car. My heartbeat started to slow. I kept my tissues in a separate pouch in my purse. The back pouch had toiletries and tissues and my lip-gloss. I rifled through and couldn't find them. I sniffled.

My fingernails went along the back, hitting the seam, until they stopped on a lump. I gripped it and pulled it out. It was Magenta wrapped in a towel. It all came back to me. I had wanted a break from Silver and decided to put her in my purse, too. I looked up at Robert's porch to see him standing there with his hands in his pockets. Without a second look, I put my keys in the ignition, sniffled, and drove off. I didn't need to apologize to him. I just needed to go home. I didn't need Robert. I didn't need anyone.

I was perfectly happy with Magenta and Silver.

TERESA NOELLE ROBERTS
INNER SPACE

F EAR GRIPPED HER, the kind of fear that was almost indistinguish-
able from excitement, as he explained what he was going to do to
her. This was the next step in his plan—*their* plan, really, but given
that he was the dominant, they both thought of it as *his*—to act out all
their fantasies. She'd confessed one of hers: to be caged, alone in the
dark, just a thing waiting to be used, no sensation except loneliness
and need until her owner chose to give it to her. A dark fantasy, she'd
admitted, but one that she couldn't get out of her mind.

Still, even though she'd whispered the details to him, she'd believed
the fantasy would be too hard to enact. But he had an idea. A compli-
cated, creepy idea that sent shock waves through her, panic or lust she
couldn't say.

Both, maybe.

She wanted to use her safeword, to curl up in a ball of denial, to run away. But she couldn't deny the moisture that started welling between her legs as he talked. She looked into his eyes, seeing the love and reassurance there along with the desire for control.

As ordered, she took out her contacts, put them into the lens case he held out for her. The room went blurry. She'd almost forgotten how that felt since the advent of extended-wear lenses; the blur was usually a matter of seconds these days as she changed to a new pair. When he turned away to put the lens case in a safe place, she almost panicked, unnerved by altered proportion, lack of focus.

When he turned back again, the blindfold was in his hands. (Not that she would have been sure what that black blob was if she hadn't been expecting it.)

Earthy smell of leather. Soft sheepskin over her eyes as darkness closed in. Her heart began to race, pounding against her ribs as if she were ten miles into a marathon.

The earplugs and white-noise headphones came next.

She'd rarely used earplugs, so the sensation of soft foam slipping into her ear cavity was a strange one anyway. Having him put them in—holding her head steady with one firm, reassuring hand as he did so—made it a thousand times stranger. It wasn't something she ever would have thought of as erotic, but his touch, his participation, made it another addition to the list of ways in which he'd penetrated her body.

No part of her was safe from him. She knew that already, had understood (and enjoyed) this fact for a long time, but this invasion, pleasurable only for the knowledge that he was doing it, possessing her in yet another way, proved it.

She could still hear, but everything was distant, diminished, unreal. Then he slipped the headphones into place and she could hear nothing but a vague, soothing *shush-shush* that she knew would soon fade into the background, become nothing.

Next came the mittens, big fleece ones that belonged to him, so large on her that he wrapped rope around each wrist to keep them from slipping off. At first she thought he'd put them on wrong, that the fact her thumb was in with her other fingers was an accident. When she felt him safety-pinning the thumb openings shut, though, she realized the truth: he was depriving her of the ability to use her hands in anything except the most rudimentary of ways, shutting her off, to a large extent, from her sense of touch.

Which explained why, for once, he'd not only told her to stay dressed, but specifically asked her to put on a baggy sweat suit. Nakedness would allow too much sensation. And that, paradoxically, sent a nervous but pleasurable shudder through her.

His hands on her shoulders brought her to her knees. He arranged her on all fours, smacked her on the butt to indicate "Crawl," guided her forward.

She knew where she was going. She knew the cage in the corner of the room, had gotten quite fond of it after being shut in it before for games of captive girl or bad puppy, after sucking his cock through its bars.

But that was when she'd had her eyes, her ears, her hands. Now, crawling in a silent vacuum across a carpet she couldn't feel, she panicked at the thought of being shut in as well.

Panicked and clenched with excitement at the knowledge that, despite her fear, she was doing it. For him.

For her.

The crawling brought out how swollen her lips were, how sensitive and eager her clit. She couldn't pretend she was doing this only for him, although she could imagine how hard he would be as he watched her fear, and crave, and obey.

He guided her into the cage, helped her settle. Then he secured the ropes around her wrists to opposite sides of the cage. He'd left long rope tails, so it wasn't the reassuring confinement of bondage. She could shift her hands around a bit, and she wasn't stretched into some uncomfortable but thrilling posture designed to invite kinky torments—she was just sitting there, leaning against the back of the cage, in almost the same casual way she might sit on the floor leaning on something. It was just enough to enforce that she couldn't, or at least shouldn't, touch her own body.

His lips brushed hers, a sensation startlingly strong and vivid in the absence of others. Soft skin, tickly bristles of his beard, the heat of his breath. Hints of possession and demand, and she wanted to wrap her arms around him and cling, but she couldn't.

Then she felt, rather than heard, the cage door shut.

If this was what oblivion, felt like, it felt…itchy. For what seemed like a long time, although it may have been only minutes, even seconds, all she was aware of was fierce itching, poison-ivy caliber itching in the small of her back, on her stomach, on the bottom of her left foot, itching that she was helpless to do anything about.

She reminded herself that she was helpless by choice, her own as well as his; that she could, at any time, plead for mercy or simply use her safeword because he hadn't gagged her, and because he wanted this to be hot for her in the long run, if unsettling in the short run.

Reminding herself of all those things took the edge off the itching—and sent a surge of pleasure running through her, flooding her pussy. Chosen helplessness, chosen darkness was arousing, even comforting, as long as she knew she could, in a pinch, escape it.

Not that she was sure she could speak now. That part of her brain seemed to be lost, along with sight and sound.

Underneath the blindfold, she opened her eyes, cringed at the strange sensation of shearling tickling her eyeballs. She'd been blindfolded before, by him and other lovers, but the blindfolds had always been imperfect, letting hints of light in if not actually allowing her to see anything else.

No light teased her, this time, at the blindfold's edges, just a different shade of darkness at the edge of darkness. Either the blindfold was placed just right, or he'd turned out all the lights in the room.

She opened her mind deliberately to the darkness, fell into it, counted her heartbeats until her mind stilled, honed in on the essentials. She was alone in the dark, caged and bound, waiting for him to release and claim her. In the darkness, though, he took on capitals—Him—like some leather-clad, distant, compelling master in an indifferently written, but arousing erotic novel. (For all his kinkiness, he would laugh at that pretentious capital, and she probably wouldn't tell him about it later, but it seemed right now.)

She was a thing in a cage, not fully human, denied pleasures so basic one didn't usually think of them as pleasures until they were gone: vision, touch, hearing, movement.

And she reveled in the knowledge of her nothingness, sitting alone in the dark in a cage.

Cut off from most sensory impressions, she became hyperaware of the ones allowed her. The soft shearling against her face. The touch of rope, muffled by fleece—she couldn't feel the coarseness of the hemp, but could smell its slight grassiness. The hardness of the cage floor, and of the bars she leaned against, the metallic cold that seeped through her clothes. The smell of her juices, soaking through her panties and the thick fleece of her sweats. The aching need in her wet pussy, taut nipples, swollen clit.

The hot trails of tears, running under the blindfold and down her cheeks. She wasn't sure why she was crying—she wasn't sad; was uneasy, but not actually frightened. Yes, in her current alienated state she could picture him not returning for her right away; could picture hours, even days, spent like this, in darkness, but that seemed right. Fitting.

She flicked out her tongue, caught a tear as it rolled down her cheek, savored salt. Maybe she'd be reduced to this, caged and forgotten and living off her own tears....

She laughed out loud at her own melodrama. Even with the headphones on, she could hear herself, the sound echoing through her bones like an explosion. There was no way to gauge, though, if she was chuckling quietly, as she hoped, or cackling like a lunatic on the subway.

And after the fit of laughter passed, so did the tears. She settled down, made herself as comfortable as she could, lost herself to aching and lust and occasional fits of restlessness where she squirmed just to prove to herself she still could or pressed harder against the bars to feel their cool metallic caress. The squirming intensified the ache in her nipples and between her legs, but even the desire, after a while, seemed detached, as if she were remembering sex after years of celibacy.

She counted under her breath for a while, trying to get a sense of the passage of time, but lost track of the numbers somewhere around one hundred and gave it up as a bad job, gave in to the formlessness. She slipped into a kind of trance, vividly aware of certain things—the dampness of her panties, the hunger to be touched, the different shades of black and deepest purple moving inside her eyelids—and unaware of much else.

The jar of the cage opening startled her. Hands—and they seemed like that to her, just hands, detached from anyone or anything else, untied her, then pulled her out of the cage. Hands pulled off her sweatpants, positioned her on her hands and knees, her ass raised, her knees apart. Cool air caressed her wet slit, sending shivers of anticipation and delight through her whole body.

Her mind observed the sensation dispassionately, as though she were feeling someone else's arousal, someone else's dripping, swollen cunt.

This couldn't be her body that was being touched, caressed; her ass that was being cupped and stroked; her nipples that swelled and peaked as they were fondled through fabric. She was elsewhere, in inner space where the darkness and the silence and the unwitting tears and the ache of neglected arousal lived.

Then hands gripped her hips and a cock ripped into her.

His cock. She couldn't disembody it, detach it, depersonalize it. She knew it too well, knew its girth and length, knew the way it moved inside her at this angle, pounding at her cervix. Knew the fingers that found her needy clit and circled it with the skill of familiarity, coaxing her to the brink of orgasm and then pushing her over it.

And then the darkness didn't matter because her eyes were screwed shut anyway, and the silence didn't matter because she could still hear the roar of her own blood, still hear her own cries as they spilled from her throat, and the mittens and enveloping clothes certainly didn't matter because nothing could muffle the waves of molten lava starting deep inside her cunt and pouring out.

She usually couldn't feel it when he came inside. She could see his body tense and relax, watch the ecstatic agony pass over his face, hear his grunt of pleasure, but couldn't sense the actual explosion inside her.

This time, deprived of other cues, she did, or at least imagined she did: the twitching and swelling of his cock, the hot semen boiling out of him and filling her.

She buckled under him, worn from orgasms and emotion.

Gently, he took off the headphones, the mittens and finally the blindfold.

She blinked in the light. The quiet room roared with background noises that sorted themselves into the gurgle of the antiquated furnace, teenagers clowning around in the neighbors' yard, distant cars. Someone in the neighborhood was playing rap, far enough away that she could hear only the angry rumble of the bass, and while she normally didn't care for rap, it sounded sweet.

"I love you," he said, and pulled her close, kissing and stroking her as if she'd been gone a long time and he were welcoming her home.

Which, in a sense, was true.

Pressed against his familiar, beloved body, she drank in his touch and his warm scent that suggested dried chilis and sunlight, now overlaid with sex-musk; the russet freckles on his ivory skin, the reddish hairs on his arms and chest, the sound of his breathing. She felt tears well up again, but this time she knew exactly why she was crying. Tears of relief, of release, of joy at leaving inner space and coming back to the world of the senses, the world where he waited for her.

STAN KENT

FOOT BINDING REVISITED

FEET BEG TO BE WORSHIPPED, and I am a lucky man, for I enjoy the pleasure of a Chinese girlfriend with dainty feet, a love of shoes and a playful, uninhibited sexual nature. I have four thousand years of history to thank for my good fortune. The Chinese were a kinky bunch, giving us many Taoist positions, some of which require the flexibility and agility of a Chinese acrobat to pull off; dubious aphrodisiacs from endangered species and numerous bizarre sexual practices that have stood the test of time and Communist repression.

One ancient ritual that has thankfully walked its last steps into history is foot binding—the crunching of the still-forming bones in a young girl's feet by wrapping them tightly in bandages for extended periods of time. The goal of the patriarchy was to keep the feet small and therefore sexually attractive and the women thereby constrained. It's hard to run away when the feet are hobbled. This terrible toesie torture has been banished in modern times, replaced simply by the wearing of four-inch-high stiletto heels. Honestly, as any woman who has been out on the town for drinks, dinner and dancing in a delight-fully gorgeous pair of Jimmy Choos knows, there's not much difference between foot binding and modern shoe finery, other than a good pair of fuck-me pumps costing a great deal more than a roll of bandages and the shoes being easier to slip off when the feet finally cry foul.

The basic motivation is the same—foot and leg worship as a form of sexual attraction and servitude—and while the choice to wear high heels is more voluntary than foot binding ever was, the societal pres-sure today to look sexy and desirable is a powerful form of coercion, convincing many women to slip on those skyscraper heels and suffer the pain and possible foot damage that comes from having the soles arched and the legs and ass emphasized.

Lizzie is no different in this regard, and in me she has a partner in crime, a codependent to urge on her addiction. I love shoes almost as much as she does and find myself deliriously running up my credit cards with names like Casadei, Louboutin, and Choo, all in the cause of providing a pedestal for Lizzie's gorgeous feet to be worshipped from near or far. When she slips on a pair of fuck-me pumps, she attracts attention.

Here I must admit a kinship to those ancient Chinese torturers who bound women's feet. It's not so much the covering—the shoe, the binding—as what's inside—the feet, the soles, the toes—that's the fea-ture attraction. It's a basic rule of how sexual fashion excites me. It's the whole package and how all the elements work together. The covering item, be it lingerie, stockings or even a shoe, is not the fetish, but

— 112 —

rather what it hides, and the true pleasure is what happens when the covering is removed and the treats are revealed.

And so it goes with Lizzie and me. When we prepare to go out for a night she spends hours, often with my consultation, choosing the exact combination of outer- and underwear and shoes, knowing that later she'll torture me to an extreme state of hardness just by being there, sipping a drink, nibbling on a tasty bite or performing a fanciful semi-striptease on the dance floor, often with an unsuspecting male who just can't believe his luck. Yes, if you haven't guessed it by now I am a confirmed voyeur as well as a die-hard foot fetishist, but that's another story in another book.

During amorous evenings such as these Lizzie knows that when the night has grown weak with encroaching sunlight and her feet are aching, her footsie exertions will be rewarded with a loving foot massage given by yours truly. There have been hundreds of nights in our relationship that have ended up this way, but one night not too long ago the past came full circle as ancient became modern. Lizzie had been particularly naughty on and off the dance floor. She had even disappeared for an extended period into the bathroom with some lucky guy. She was more than a bit high and full of her dominatrix side when we got home, demanding I perform her foot massage before she'd have sex, which I generally view as my reward. She slipped out of her little slip of a dress. Her thong panties were missing in action—that lucky guy's souvenir. She stood there in thigh-high Wolford white stockings and four-inch Christian Louboutin black lace-up, open-toed, stiletto platforms. She was to die for and she knew it. I would give her what she wanted.

"Lie down on the bed," I said.

She fell backward, her legs dangling off the bed. I grabbed her ankles and rolled her facedown. She flopped over rag doll–like. I bent her legs at the knee and unlaced the shoes, staring at her beautiful heart-shaped ass that served as the most exquisite backdrop for my visual treat. After the shoes were unlaced and off, I rolled down the silky-soft stockings, taking my time to enjoy the subtle differentiation between Lizzie's silky soft skin and the luxurious material. Lizzie was enjoying the attention too. I had a feeling that the bathroom encounter, while thrilling, had left her in a supreme state of cunty readiness. Her hands were under her body, working feverishly between her legs. I saw the dart of jet-black fingernails flicking through the folds of her pussy. She was moaning and moving her ass up and down. Oh, how she loves a good foot massage.

As I rolled the stockings off her feet I pulled them from her toes, noticing an amazing symmetry gaping at me from across the ages. I felt an immediate bond with those Chinese patriarchs of centuries ago. Lizzie's feet were clasped together, the arches producing a small opening through which, in her facedown, ass-up pose, I saw her pussy winking back at me. The basic shapes were identical, and through the folds of history I understood one of the perverse reasons for foot binding—small feet, when clasped together, produce a beautiful surrogate pussy. I was possessed with a demonlike desire to plunder Lizzie's foot-pussy. I held her size-5 feet together at the ankles and knotted the stockings around them, completing the bondage at the toes.

"What are you doing?" Lizzie asked.

"Binding your feet."

"Oh," Lizzie said as if I did so every day. The woman is amazing in her ability to absorb sexual kink in stride. It also helped that she was Chinese, drunk and more than a little disorderly.

I hopped off the bed, struggling out of my clothes. I grabbed the bottle of cinnamon massage oil that we keep by the bed for our rub-downs and rechargings. The silky liquid warms with stroking to supposedly ease all those muscle aches, but I had another use in mind. It was going to be my surrogate pussy's surrogate pussy juice. I was back on the bed with a Flying Dagger–like leap and behind Lizzie's stocking-bound feet before she could say "Fuck my little piggies." Somewhere in time an ancient old Chinese pervert was smiling on me. Who knows, maybe it was karma, and I was the reincarnation of some Chinese Emperor and Lizzie was my favorite concubine and we were simply acting out what we had done all those centuries ago.

I poured a flood of oil over Lizzie's toes, catching the drips in my palms as I worked the oil into and around her feet, careful to avoid the surrogate pussy of her compressed arches. I was teasing her the way she likes her pussy to be touched, communicating with her body in the manner she prefers and is familiar with, telegramming the message that her feet were her pussy. In normal foreplay she doesn't like me to dive right into her cunt, but to spiral in from her silky thighs, working her into a frenzy of anticipation. And this I did with her feet, knead-ing, squeezing, stroking, gradually working my way to her opening. I poured more oil on my hands and worked it into her arches, liberally coating the bottoms of her feet. Where her arches came together near the toes I flicked my finger as I might on her clit, then slid my fingers inside her soles, working my fingers into what would have been her

— 115 —

G-spot, but was actually the balls of her feet. Lizzie giggled as some of the touches were tickling. She writhed on her fingers, and my fingers mirrored what she was doing to her pussy. It was a riveting sight and sensation, and my cock responded with a steely hardness.

Fuck the footie foreplay, I couldn't wait any longer. I poured oil on my erection and straightened my body, inserting my cock between her feet, which I clasped tightly together, adding the pressure of my hands to the stocking binding. The warmth of the oil radiated from her skin to my cock. It was as if I were in her pussy, with one major differ-ence—with each thrust I was greeted with the sight of my cockhead emerging through the tight folds of Lizzie's foot-pussy. When we fuck in the normal way I love watching my shaft sliding in and out of her tight little pussy, with her labial flesh gripping at me as if her pussy were reluctant to let my cock leave; now I was treated to the sight of my cockhead popping out from the other side of her sole-sex, giving me double the usual sensation of entry and exit. As my swollen head forced its way out of the compress of Lizzie's feet, only to be pulled back so that the sensitive rim was rubbed against her oily soles, the undulations of her skin added a feeling remarkably like that of her pussy's clutch, but amplified. I had never experienced anything like this. I was entranced by the sight, feel and sound of my cock sliding in and out of Lizzie's foot-pussy, the smell of the massage oil and the muskiness of feet that have been out all night. I was on erotic overload, and while I was lost in the newness of my foot-sex discoveries, Lizzie was beyond control with what I was doing to her. The sensations of my cock were tickling her feet, making her writhe, which she com-pounded with expert manipulations of her fingers in her pussy. I would not let her escape, holding her legs tight against me. When she comes, Lizzie often bursts into unrestrained laughter as all those tightly bound emotions burst forth. Now add to that the comic aspects of a foot-fucking and she was deliriously in a near-constant state of climaxing.

Watching her come and come again made it impossible to hold myself beyond a few more minutes' worth of stroking my cock into her foot-pussy. Her feet could not be denied me. She had teased me all night long, and this was my reward. I thrust into her, pulling her feet into my crotch, squeezing my tender cockhead out of her soles as I orgasmed, shooting a stream of milky come all along her back and into her raven tresses.

I held my come-sensitized cock in that position until I had the fortitude to withdraw. I so enjoyed the sensation of her warm feet against my tingling shaft that I continued the massaging with my softening cock until it grew hard again, and then, keeping Lizzie's feet bound, I straddled her body and fucked her from the rear, completing the foot-pussy circuit with a frenetic fuck of her well-fingered pussy from between her closely bound thighs.

Since that time foot-pussy play has become a staple of our sexual diet. We have expanded our repertoire to include intricate bondage. In addition to touch-heating massage oil we keep lengths of rope by our bed. I bind Lizzie's calves and ankles and toes together to form a foot-pussy, and then I tie her arms to the bed so she can't touch herself, but I strap a vibrating egg massager to her pussy to drive her wild. Foot-fuck possibilities are endless. Lizzie is limber enough that it is possible to vary the position, with her lying on her back so she can see my cock fucking her feet and the look on my face as I come, shooting a pearl necklace across her breasts.

We've invited others to join us in our foot binding revisited, and that's led to toe-sucking and cock-licking being added to our foot-fucking. Given the success of those encounters we've hosted foot-pussy parties, satisfying my voyeurism and foot fetishes in one decadent evening.

The ancient Chinese art of reflexology is based upon the notion that the soles of the feet are connected through meridian lines to vital organs, and through appropriate pressure during foot massage, any ailment can be cured. In Lizzie's case I think her feet must be connected directly to her pussy and the erotic center of her brain, for I've never seen anyone so consumed by pleasure and full of life as she is when her feet are being fucked.

RACHEL KRAMER BUSSEL

FISHNET QUEEN

IRST THING I SEE ARE HER LEGS, clad in the kind of stockings that make me hard just from thinking about them: fishnets. Her legs are long, and in her miniskirt, which rides up her thigh, I can see her pale skin augmented by the tightly woven black pattern that seems made just for her. She doesn't just wear the fishnets, she *owns* them. I've seen women try to rock fishnets who simply can't pull it off, who wear them as if they were any other kind of stockings, tugged on hastily during a rushed morning, ripped in spots, slammed into sneakers, used and abused in the most careless manner possible.

There should be some kind of test for those purchasing such delicate garments, I think, like showing ID for cigarettes, but in all things fishnet, the test should be for class. I can always tell when a woman really cares about her fishnets, when she's the type who shakes them out before holding open the hole and sliding her foot into it, aware of every nuance of sensuality involved. I can tell when she makes sure that the seam up the back is perfectly even, forming a straight line right up to her ass, one I love to trace with my tongue; when she cares enough to buy the kind that have a seam. I can tell when the mere act of donning a pair of fishnets sends a rush of blood to her clit, when she morphs from gorgeous to goddess in the act, when she lets them transport her from ordinary to sex goddess. The rest of her outfit doesn't really matter, nor how tall or short she is; a woman who wears fishnets like they're her birthright is the kind I want to fuck, the kind whose fishnets I want to kiss and stroke and caress before ultimately peeling them down and plunging my cock inside her. Fishnet girls are all about foreplay, leaving me on the edge of arousal for as long as we both can stand it. That's the kind of woman I look for, who wears her fishnets not simply as artifice or armor but amour, who steps into her dominance one foot at a time.

This particular fishnet queen is sitting in the corner of my favorite local café in a plush chair, with another chair facing her, so I assume she's with someone. I'm disappointed but still thrilled to have gotten even a glimpse of her as I head to the counter to order my latte, one eye on those legs just because they're there. Only once I've gotten my steaming brew do I see the rest of her, a mop of ink-black hair inelegantly tossed against her head, eyes painted with kohl, some kind of black outfit, black sweater, dark nails. I bet she's the kind of girl who only wears high-fashion black, the kind of fabrics that melt to the touch, who spends a fortune on her underwear and stockings and keeps them constantly updated, and if she's not, I'd be more than happy to keep her stocked in fishnets.

She looks up, as if searching for a waiter, though this isn't the kind of place with table service. Her eyes meet mine and she raises her brow. I practically trip toward her when she cocks her head. I should be used to women who wear fishnets making the first move, but I grew up in a time and place where, sadly, that was the man's job. The first time a woman (older, my college roommate's mom, of course) put her hand on my ass in a way that wasn't joking or asking but taking what was clearly hers, I practically came in my pants. It's only a very specific kind of woman who makes me long to get down on my knees and worship my way from the tips of her toes all the way on up, and the fishnets are just a part of it.

This stranger has a look in her eye letting me know she meets guys like me all the time. The idea that I'm no one special, that she's inviting me over because she knows exactly what I want and is waiting to see if I'll make the grade, has me standing taller and walking with more authority. I want to prove myself to her before we've even met, prove that I can be whoever she wants me to be, whenever she wants me to be. It doesn't make sense but, like the best sexual encounters, it doesn't have to. It's not something you think about, but something you feel from the tip of your tongue down the back of your throat right on down to your hard, throbbing cock—at least, that's how it is for me.

"Sit," she says before taking a sip of the steaming coffee in her mug. It's straight black, fittingly, in a room where almost everyone else has some tongue twister of a five-dollar beverage poised against his or her manicured hands. Up close, I see her nails aren't exactly black, but a glossy, gleaming red so dark it takes being next to it to appreciate its bloodlike hue. The image makes me think of her clawing at me with the nails, on the edge of drawing blood, but I look up into her brown eyes instead as I place myself into the plush chair opposite her. Then I sit holding my coffee, waiting for her reaction, her next command, as my loafered feet land perilously close to her heels. Even just having that one part of me near her legs makes my cock jolt, and I shift in my seat, wanting to hide my hardness from her, at least until we're introduced.

She sips her coffee, appraising me, and I marvel at her ability to look not only like she owns this place, but like that would be a worthy feat. Almost all the other patrons are tucked into themselves, hovered over laptops or notebooks, ears curled into cell phones, bent down to blow on their hot beverages. She sits proudly, her legs grabbing all the attention as she does whatever calculations she needs to do. "Name?" she asks, like she's on a fact-finding mission.

I could lie, but I don't. "Brad," I say, the lone syllable sounding inadequate somehow. I wish it were more stately, elegant, befitting someone about to join such a queen, but it is what it is.

"Hmmm…" is all she says, looking me over. Then her shoe clatters to the ground and her foot hovers near me. I can see bright red toenails peeking out of the mesh. I'm torn between wanting to press her fishnet-covered foot against my face and easing them off to suck on her toes directly. "You want to be down there, don't you, Brad?" she asks, leaning forward and almost sloshing her dark brew onto me.

She grabs my wrist and those strong nails dig into the underside. My dick is rock hard and I'm afraid I'll come in my pants. She knows, somehow. Maybe it's obvious, maybe anyone looking can see by my face, my posture, everything about me that I want nothing more right now than to be kneeling next to her, my tongue between her legs, fishnets on either side, buried in her cunt. She reaches up to pinch my bottom lip, twisting it until it hurts. It's the good kind of hurt, don't worry; she knows exactly how to play me even though we've just met. That's another thing about real fishnet queens; they can read me like an open book. They don't need elaborate instructions or yes/no lists or safewords. They get it, just like that.

"What would you give to be between my legs right now? What can you offer me that will make me take you home with me?" Part of me wants to look around, see if anyone's heard her, make sure this is actually happening. But she's moved her fingers back to my wrist, grabbing it forcefully. She shifts so her knee just lightly brushes mine. My mind races to find the right answer, the perfect gift. I know it's not money she wants; that would be way too pedestrian for the likes of her.

"I can offer you a lifetime supply of stockings. Fishnets in particular," I say, the idea coming to me from some deep recess of my brain. How much could they cost, really? Okay, I know the answer to that, I know that the high-end ones she probably prefers can run a pretty penny, but she's worth it, that much I know. "As many as you want…as long as you let me put them on you," I add, daring to tack on a condition that just may kill our negotiation.

"I'll want that in writing," she says, letting go of my arm and sinking back into her seat. She takes a satisfied sip and then turns back to the magazine she'd been reading. I look away, drink my coffee but barely taste it. I keep my eyes cast down at my hands, my lap, nothing. If I look up I'll surely blush or encounter prying eyes, and to look at her would be rude, would breach what little trust she's granted me. I sip slowly, draw it out, until she's done. I don't have a watch so I don't know how long it takes, but I try to relax and just bask in her presence. I've been waiting to meet someone just like her, have taken out ads and gone on blind dates and even prayed, but here she is, as if she were waiting just for me.

"Get up," she snaps, her steely voice reminding me that my hard-on still hasn't subsided. I rise quickly, and she hands me her bag to carry while her heels click on the tiles. She does have seams running up the backs of her fishnets, and a slit in her skirt that gives me a glimpse of smooth thighs. I hope someday I'll get to grab her from behind, get to bend her over and press my legs against her stockinged legs while I slide my dick inside her again and again. I know we're a long way away from that, but marching behind her brings that image to the fore.

I don't know where I'm going and for the first time in a long time, I don't need to. People think that submission is easy, and in a sense it is. You get to be the one following orders, not giving them. Yet it's such a departure from my daily routine, where decisions must be made every moment, where a ringing phone is my constant companion, where one wrong move could cost millions. Here all I have to do is listen to her words as they emerge from her plump red lips while I imagine what she will want to do to me. It's an adjustment I'm happy to make. Her driver is outside in a limo waiting to take us where she needs to go.

He doesn't even bat an eye when I hold the door for her and hurry in afterward. "You know where to go," she tells him. She may as well be telling me; I know, too. "Turn around," she says, twirling her finger to let me know she wants me looking out the window. I do, but only for a moment, before she slips a blindfold over my eyes. For a moment, I wonder if this is dangerous, if my instincts have led me astray, if I'll wind up dead or abandoned somewhere. Then I feel her fingers pressing against the back of my neck, digging and massaging all at once, the same way she did to my wrist. I let out the breath I've been holding.

"We're both going to get what we want, Brad," she says, her use of my name making me realize I don't know hers. "You don't need to know who I am right now. There's time for that later. Right now you're going to service me and if you do a good job, maybe you'll be rewarded." I feel her at my wrists again and realize she's binding them. She's not using rope, though, and as she tugs the bonds against my arms, I realize she's used a pair of fishnets! I haven't heard any rustling to signal she's removed her own, so she must have had a spare pair somewhere. Once again I almost come, but manage to hold off.

"What do you want, Brad?" she asks, even though she's gotta know. Her lips rush to my neck, then my ear, her teeth biting none too gently. Her fingers tickle my cock, the nails gracing its hardness with the lightest of touches.

"I want to lick your pussy. I want you to wet my face with your juices. I want to make you come again and again," I say, the words getting raspier as I hear them hover in the air. They sound so much dirtier when spoken aloud, especially since we're not alone, but they're totally true.

"You better do a good job," she says, and I smile just for a second, because if there's one thing I'm good at, it's eating pussy. I've always loved the sensual feel of being trapped between a woman's thighs, her musk wafting around me, my tongue sliding against her oyster, lapping at the pearl, and diving back inside. I could spend hours between a woman's legs, and I have, but I know we don't have that kind of time. The car's been zipping smoothly along, making occasional turns. My wrists are snug between the fishnets, and I wonder if they're ones she's worn before, wonder whether they contain the traces of her juices. She guides me between her legs, her skirt hiked up. She's splayed out against the seat while I'm scrunched down, but the minute I get a taste of her, none of that matters. She's not wearing any panties, and the fishnet tights travel all the way up, so between the small holes of the fabric, my tongue meets her slippery, salty flesh. I push harder, feeling the slight abrasion of the fabric against my tongue. She must like the rough sensation as I lick my way up. Her hand clamps to the back of my head, tugging at the short hairs there. I try to ignore my aching cock as I savor her cream.

I nuzzle my face from side to side, and while I'm blissfully between her lips, I forget that we've just met, that all I really know about her is what she wears and what she drinks and what she tastes like. That's all I need as I work my tongue against the fishnets' grooves, loving it yet longing to plunge all the way inside. She's groaning against me, shoving my face deeper into her pussy, until she finally pushes me back and tears a hole in the tights just big enough to let me inside. I'm surrounded by her labia and the wet tights; in other words, I'm in heaven.

She's rocking up against me and getting wetter and wetter, practically shoving her cunt into my mouth and I love every second of it. "Fuck me with your tongue, Brad," she screams, and that's exactly what I do, the scratchy tights lightly abrading my cheeks. I know I will feel and taste her later even if this is my only chance, and that spurs me on. I've been trying not to rush things, not to go too fast as I press against her walls, rotating my tongue against the places that are most sensitive. I pull out and suck on her clit, wishing for the use of my fingers even though my body delights in the bondage she's put me in. I breathe warmly against her clit, feel it stiffen even more, then tap my tongue against it steadily. Then harder and harder, *flick, flick, flick,* until she's using me as her fuck toy, slamming my mouth against her pussy over and over again, sliding up and down, grinding against me. There are moments when I can barely breathe, and those are the ones I love the most. I am my fishnet queen's pussy slave, here for her pleasure, and she takes and takes and takes, coming against me not once or even twice but three times, leaving me coated with her essence.

I'm sure the blindfold is probably ruined too, and when she guides me out from between her legs and takes it off, I stare up at her, my eyes glossy, glazed with lust. My cock is still hard but no longer so insistent; I've been in a place where my pleasure was subsumed by hers. She still manages to look regal even with her torn stockings and reddened cheeks. "Sit back against the window," she says, and I do, feeling my bound hands press against the door, my head tilted to the chilled window. I can see her deep pink pussy lips from here. She stretches her legs out toward me, and I quickly see where this is going. She rubs my cock with one fishnet-covered foot, then, impatient, leans forward to let my naked shaft emerge. Her foot upon my cock is an image that will be permanently seared into my mind. Hard, straining red dick against tender black; glimpses of her pale skin beneath. Her foot is warm and soft, and when she brings the other one around to manipulate me between them, I'm gone. The woven fabric against my hot flesh makes me spurt, both of us watching as a river of come erupts from my cock onto her feet.

My face contorts as a few tears trickle down my face, done in by the sheer relief of a fantasy not just fulfilled but exceeded in every possible way. That's when she takes off the fishnets, the ones soiled with both of our orgasms, and shoves them in my mouth. I breathe deeply through my nose while she fishes out some papers, makes some notations. "Sign these," she says, handing me a pen. She's somehow filled out a contract cementing our plan. I look at her in awed fascination. I've never met a woman like her before, and probably never will again. I see the car swinging back to our original meeting place, and I quickly scrawl my signature. "Put your phone number, too." I do, but again, she doesn't give me hers. "Meet me here next week, same time, same place." She hands me a slip of paper with a brand name and make on it. They're one of the priciest hosiery companies around, and seeing the words makes my cock twitch. I wonder if I'll be able to get home from the store without jerking off. She pulls the ball of sodden fishnets from my lips, and I whimper. "Keep them," she says, leaning over to open the car door, her breasts brushing my lap as she does. I get out, dazed, surely looking foolish as I clutch her instructions and her tights in my hands while the limo departs. I don't dare go back inside, but start walking, with two miles to go, her fishnets in my hands to remind me that this wasn't a dream.

ALISON TYLER

VIEW FROM PARIS

T HE VIEW FROM THE BALCONY overlooking Paris's residential 13th
Arrondissement took in romantic rooftops, a breathtaking candy-
pink sunset, and a lone young man in a firecracker-red T-shirt
watching the two of us with unwavering interest. Josh saw him first.
"Look down, Lanie," he said, his hand under the strap of my gauzy
silver nightgown. "Over there…"

I looked in the direction he was indicating, and that's exactly the
moment when Josh slid the straps over my bare arms and pulled my
forties-style movie-star nightgown past my naked breasts to the curve
of my hips.

"Josh…" I said, crossing my arms over my full breasts. "He's
watching."

"That's what I was telling you," my new husband said, nuzzling
the back of my neck as his hands removed mine from my breasts. His

fingers took over, teasing my nipples as he continued to kiss along the nape of my neck. "He's been there every evening."

And so had we.

This was our new tradition, to slip into nightclothes in the late afternoon, waking just when the sun went down to catch a sunset romp out on the balcony. We'd felt exposed, yet oddly protected, being up on the fifth floor of the apartment we'd rented for our honeymoon. Now I knew that we weren't protected at all. Josh seemed thrilled by this prospect, and as his fingers relentlessly played over my breasts, I relaxed into the idea, as well. We were in Paris, after all. Nobody knew us. None of our normal, everyday activities were in play here. Our entire routine was topsy-turvy in the most pleasurable way. We no longer started our morning with a healthy meal of oatmeal and OJ. In Paris, we had croissants at ten, then lingered over filling lunches around one, not bothering to even think about dinner until nine in the evening. At the time of day when we'd usually be facing rush hour traffic, we made love.

Now Josh moved to my side and turned me so that I was facing him. We were still easily visible to our naughty neighbor, and I kept that in mind as Josh began to kiss my breasts. He used one hand to palm my right tit while he suckled from the left. Then he switched activities, so no part of my body felt left out. As his mouth worked me over, I thought about the scene we'd admired the night before. Josh had suggested an evening at The Crazy Horse, and we'd enjoyed the erotic art of the women dancing and exposing themselves to us. Was I crazy enough on Paris's open attitudes to let myself be a woman on display? It seemed that I was.

When I didn't protest, or try to pull Josh back into the apartment, he slowly undid the tie at the back of my nightgown that held the dainty fabric in place at my hips. With one pull of the lace, the nightgown slid in a ripple of lovely silk to my ankles. Here I was, a woman of satiny skin and curves, bathed in the pink glow of the heavens and admired by two sets of eyes: my husband's and those of the man in the bright red shirt. And while I've always adored being on display for my man, it was the stranger's eyes that made me tremble.

Who was he? What did he think about my body? Was he turned on by my feminine curves or by Josh's hard and lean physique?

These thoughts and a multitude of others were still running through my mind when Josh bent me over the railing and began to kiss between my thighs from behind. I felt the slight breath of cool evening air surround me and the warmth of his tongue and lips against my pussy. The sensations were intensely arousing—being outside while behaving in the most intimate of ways has always been a turn-on for me, a fantasy I don't usually get to indulge in. Josh and I live in such a small town that the disgrace of being caught playing in public would be too much to live down. Too much for us to ever get more frisky than a little petting in a parking lot every once in a while.

But we weren't in our small town anymore. We were in Paris, and I gazed into the room owned by a stranger and imagined I could see the yearning in his face, the desire in his eyes, the bulge in his slacks.

Josh made me thoroughly wet with his naughty kissing games, and then he stood and slid his pajama bottoms down, parted my thighs, and entered me. I closed my eyes for one moment, basking in the dreamy feeling of being taken by my husband. But I had to open them again quickly so that I could stare at our audience. I've read that when you're on stage, you're supposed to choose one person to focus on, and do your show for that single selected audience member. I'd chosen mine, and he seemed deeply honored, leaning into his windowsill, anxious to catch every act of our very personal show.

My handsome husband fucked me from behind for as long as he could take it, and then turned me around, lifting me into his embrace and bouncing me up and down on his glorious cock. I couldn't watch from this position, but I didn't mind. I could feel the stranger's eyes on my body, and my pussy responded by tightening and releasing rapidly, connecting with Josh, contracting on him.

When I came, it was as if there were three of us right there on the balcony: me and Josh and a man whose name I didn't know, but whose willing participation took me higher than I ever had been before. I cried out, not bothering to try to stifle the sounds of my pleasure, and Josh responded by coming right away, holding me tightly to his body as he filled me up. We stayed connected, my legs around his waist, until a shiver ran through me and Josh set me down on the tiny balcony once again.

As I reached for my discarded nightgown, I thought about our choices for honeymoon locations, and our decision to come to Paris, a place renowned for its sights. It turns out the most exciting view Paris had to offer was us.

ABOUT THE EDITOR

CALLED "A TROLLOP WITH A LAPTOP" by *East Bay Express*, and a "literary siren" by Good Vibrations, Alison Tyler is naughty and she knows it. Ms. Tyler is the author of more than twenty explicit novels, including *Learning to Love It*, *Strictly Confidential*, *Sweet Thing*, *Sticky Fingers*, *Something About Workmen, Rumors*, *Tiffany Twisted* and *With or Without You* (Cheek). Her short stories have appeared in more than seventy anthologies and have been translated into Spanish, German, Italian, Japanese, Greek and Dutch.

She is the editor of thirty-five anthologies including *Heat Wave*, *Best Bondage Erotica* volumes 1 & 2, *The Merry XXXMas Book of Erotica*, *Luscious*, *Red Hot Erotica*, *Slave to Love*, *Three-Way*, *Happy Birthday Erotica* (all from Cleis Press); *Naughty Fairy Tales from A to Z* (Plume); and the *Naughty Stories from A to Z* series, the *Down & Dirty* series,

Naked Erotica and *Juicy Erotica* (all from Pretty Things Press). Please visit www.prettythingspress.com.

Ms. Tyler is loyal to coffee (black), lipstick (red), and tequila (straight). She has tattoos, but no piercings; a wicked tongue, but a quick smile; and bittersweet memories, but no regrets. She believes it won't rain if she doesn't bring an umbrella, prefers hot and dry to cold and wet, and loves to spout her favorite motto: "You can sleep when you're dead." She chooses Led Zeppelin over the Beatles, the Cure over the Smiths, and the Stones over everyone—yet although she appreciates good rock, she has a pitiful weakness for '80s hair bands.

In all things important, she remains faithful to her partner of over a decade, but she still can't choose just one perfume.